"Did you ever think, cowboy, this change in your niece is kinda due to you, too?"

Nick liked the idea, even if she was saying it just to please him. Then a drop of rain fell, followed by another until the flash storms so frequent in Spring left them both wet to the skin and running for the hotel.

Two minutes later he was bidding her goodnight.

"Goodnight, cowboy." She smiled.

He paused, then pressed a kiss, hot and firm, on her mouth. She tasted of scotch and strawberries and before she could brush him off, he straightened and nodded. "Goodnight, then."

She hesitated for only a moment and closed the door.

He stood, staring at her door a second too long, wishing he had said how he felt.

Dear Reader,

I was home for the holidays when I saw the call for Westerns. A Desire blitz...with the promise of editorial feedback! My youngest, Matilda, was responsible for the sleep deprivation that motivated me to challenge myself, and I'm so glad I did!

I loved every moment spent creating *Montana Legacy*: the vast beauty of Montana, the complicated hero, the deception and drama accompanying generational wealth and a leading lady with a secret!

Rose and Nick are united in grief, finding in each other a connection forged through loss and compassion. I took a risk introducing a sixteen-year-old orphan as a strong secondary character, but I loved the layered conflict Alix brought to the story and, I must admit, she reminds me of my little sister, Trish—spunky, clever and independent.

Rose, who previously lacked direction in her life, identifies with Alix, determined to mentor the girl and falling for her brooding uncle in the process. Nick? Despite swearing to keep things strictly business, the new tutor is intoxicating...

I can't wait for you to read it.

Bisous from the Alps,

Katie

Please say hi: Instagram, @romanceinthealps; Goodreads and Bookbub, Katie_Frey; or, more embarrassingly, TikTok, @romanceinthealps.

KATIE FREY

MONTANA LEGACY

HARLEQUIN®

DESIRE™

ISBN-13: 978-1-335-73560-7

Montana Legacy

Copyright © 2022 by Kaitlin Muddiman Frey

Recycling programs
for this product may
not exist in your area.

This is a work of fiction. Names, characters, places and incidents
are either the product of the author's imagination or are used fictitiously.
Any resemblance to actual persons, living or dead, businesses,
companies, events or locales is entirely coincidental.

For questions and comments about the quality of this book,
please contact us at CustomerService@Harlequin.com.

Harlequin Enterprises ULC
22 Adelaide St. West, 41st Floor
Toronto, Ontario M5H 4E3, Canada
www.Harlequin.com

Printed in U.S.A.

Katie Frey has spent the better part of her adult life in pursuit of her own happily-ever-after. Said pursuit involved international travel and a few red herrings before she moved from Canada to Switzerland to marry her own mountain man.

Katie is a member of the RWA and an avid writer, and *Montana Legacy* is her first novel for Harlequin Desire. She wrote the bulk of the book in a local coffee shop. Any excuse to stay near the fresh croissants!

She is most active on Instagram, @romanceinthealps, but you can also find her on Facebook at Kate Frey Writes, on Goodreads and Bookbub or, most embarrassingly, on TikTok, @romanceinthealps. The communication she's most proud of however, is her newsletter, which you can join at bit.ly/3COLHoP.

Books by Katie Frey

Harlequin Desire

Montana Legacy

Visit her Author Profile page at Harlequin.com, or romanceinthealps.com, for more titles.

You can also find Katie Frey on Facebook, along with other Harlequin Desire authors, at www.Facebook.com/harlequindesireauthors!

I'd like to dedicate my first Harlequin novel to my mom, who never doubted for a second it would exist.

One

"Look, I'm just saying, maybe it's time you came home."

Nick Hartmann raised his voice as he adjusted the Bluetooth volume settings on the steering wheel of his Nissan Titan Platinum pickup truck. The clock on the dashboard blinked a foreboding reminder he was late, and he leaned on the gas in answer.

"I'm not coming home, Nick," Jackson snapped, his refusal ringing throughout the truck. "I'm on circuit for the season. Look, I signed the power of attorney—just make a decision and keep sending the checks." Nick's younger brother's voice was partially obscured by the roaring soundscape of a lively party. Nick tightened his grip on the steering wheel until his fingernails dug into the leather. He was tired of being the only Hartmann to know his brother's alias, which he apparently needed for riding rodeo, although it was a small price to pay for the extra vote on the board. Of course, even with Jackson's vote, Nick had held a minority voice in the face of their three siblings. Until now. Now it was two siblings against two siblings, with a swing vote no one saw coming.

The sun was rising on a new era for the Hartmanns.

"So Austin, Katherine… Alix?" Nick started, choking on the names. "It doesn't change anything?"

"No. These broncos aren't going to ride themselves. Plus, I don't see what my coming back can do for anyone at this point." It was a cavalier dismissal. *Very Jackson.*

"It'd be nice to have you back, Jacks," Nick tried again. If he stood a shot at convincing his brother to do anything, honesty was the best policy. In the four years since their father died, Jackson hadn't so much as seen the grass seed on the plot where they'd buried Dad. Sure, the deathbed argument had been a bad one. But his dad was gone, and instead of helping with the ranch, Jacks had checked out the day their dad died. Jackson's exit he could understand. Nick supposed it was easier to feel like less of a disappointment without facing the headstone of the man who'd labeled him as such.

Of course, Jackson wasn't the first Hartmann to leave. Austin had scorched the earth like an enemy trailblazer sixteen years ago, leaving with Katherine of all people. She'd been Nick's high school sweetheart, and, he grimaced with the memory, his first love. Even now, close on two decades later, he didn't know what had hurt more: Austin leaving, or the fact that he took Katherine away, too.

Yep. First Austin, then Jackson. Now, with Evie living in California, only Amelia, the bossy twin, was left to fight with him. Nick Hartmann was the only one left who wanted to keep this ranch intact.

Until now, if he played his cards right.

"You wanted to be in charge, big brother, and now you got it." Without ceremony, Jackson disconnected. *Honesty indeed.*

Nick stared ahead, wondering if it was true, the cars he followed zooming out of focus. *Had he wanted this?*

Only now, in the solitude of his new truck, was he ready to admit how he'd felt when his older brother Austin's name flashed on his cell phone at four a.m. last week. Annoyed.

The annoyance was followed by shock upon realizing it wasn't his estranged brother on the other end of the line, but a hospital administrator. Austin and his wife, Katherine, were dead on the scene of a helicopter crash. At least, per the hospital, the deaths had been quick and clean.

The feelings crescendoed; then guilt sang the loudest of them all. The guilt was still with him, a punishment for the few seconds he'd wished Austin hadn't woken him up.

The guilt deepened when Saul Kellerman, the family's lawyer, called the following day with the news that Nick had been designated guardian of Alix, his sixteen-year-old niece. A niece he had never met. Then came the silver lining—impossible to ignore and disgusting to recognize. As her guardian, Nick would vote in her stead at the family's company for two years, until she came of age. As long as Nick maintained custody of Alix, the tides would turn. And so the two votes, his and Jackson's, became three. Austin's child, the unwitting pendulum swinging favor to the coalition of siblings set on saving the ranch.

Nick was now the head of the new majority.

But his plan had one weak point. The kid. Austin naming him the guardian of his and Katherine's daughter was salt in the wound, inexplainable, but also an opportunity.

In two years, she'd vote on her own, and if she hated the ranch? Hated him? The two years could flip from a saving grace to a paltry stay of execution if he didn't manage them right. Nick swallowed his feelings, his guilt, amplified in the heat of his truck. The kid looked like Katherine. Hard to pretend she didn't. But looking like his lying ex-girlfriend was hardly an excuse for turning his back on her. She was a kid. No, he was going to do right by Alix. Nick knew exactly how it felt to be abandoned by family, and he wasn't about to do the same thing to a kid, despite her parents. In spite of Austin and whatever agenda he'd issued from beyond the grave, Nick would do the right thing for Alix and the ranch.

The best for Alix started with the best education money could buy, in the form of a world-class tutor. No one could say he was cutting corners, not even the ghost of his father. A live-in tutor was a surefire plan to help Alix fall in love with the land that ran through her blood. Commuting forty minutes to high school was not a selling point for most adolescents, and the last thing he wanted was another boarding school. No, the tutor was a key part of his plan.

Nick frowned at the signs. The tutor cleared customs in Denver, so she'd arrive at the domestic terminal. *He just might make it in time.*

Nick tilted his hat back, an action so familiar it was reflexive, and drew a hand along his jaw, rubbing the stubble as he slowed on the arrivals ramp. He didn't see her.

He stayed on the ramp, circling to take another pass, this time slowing to a crawl for the second try. There was only one woman standing at column ten and it wasn't the tutor. Couldn't be. He had hired a world-class teacher, multidisciplined and Oxford-educated. He wanted someone beyond reproach, education being a crucial element of guardianship. This woman didn't look old enough to have a teaching degree, much less bear the accolades advertised by the recruitment agency. Yet she leaned against the column, standing precisely under a clearly marked ten, and there was no one else in the vicinity. Two bags—a large canvas rucksack and a beat-up suitcase—were lined up beside her. He slowed, and rolled down the window, offering a cautious, "Mary Kelly?"

Her head shot up, and his inquiry was met with a smile. Cobalt eyes blinked at him from under a tousle of fat blond ringlets. Bedroom hair. He swallowed, dry-mouthed at the sight of her. The schoolmarm cardigan did little to disguise her figure, which was as tempting as her bee-stung lips. This was not what he'd had in mind when he'd put the wheels of homeschooling in motion. The goal was to get the kid to fall in love with Montana, not for him to fall in lust with her tutor.

"Yes?" Her curls bounced as she skipped toward him and put a tentative hand on the door handle.

Nick was out of the car in a flash, circling around to offer his help.

She was pretty, this tutor, but boy did it intensify when she flashed a smile in his direction. It had been a while since he'd been struck by an initial attraction so visceral. *It was a problem.* The last thing he needed around the ranch right now was another attractive employee temptation. He'd made poor enough decisions in that arena as it stood. If he wanted to keep custody of Alix, thus winning the vote as her proxy and reversing the family's recent vote to sell the ranch, he needed to be a suitable guardian. One who didn't just hire tempting tutors, but proper educators.

True to form, airport parking authorities passed his truck, blue lights flashing. "Mr. Hartmann, good to see you," the man said through an open window, offering a smile in their direction.

Mary paled. "Mr. Hartmann?" she asked.

His smile widened. "Yep." He paused, and lifted his hat briefly before putting it back square on his head. "And you're Mary Kelly?" He frowned and cleared his throat. "I'm surprised, that's all. You're a tutor? The Oxford-graduate tutor?"

Perhaps it was rude to lace each word with accusation, but he didn't care. Mary Kelly looked more like an Instagram influencer than a tutor, and he needed to be sure.

She bristled. "Look, it's been a long day. I'm on the other side of two red-eye flights and a bloody crap connection in Denver, and now what precisely are you saying? That I don't *look* like a tutor?" Her posh voice shook with irritation, and she eyed him narrowly.

It had been a long time since someone had talked back to Nick. And in all that time, he hadn't had any idea what he'd been missing, because the sass aimed his way was more refreshing than an aged Scotch. He stood in stunned silence, fighting back a blush of his own, a feeling as unfamiliar as it was arousing.

"Did you ever think, *sir*, perhaps *you* don't look like a rancher?" she fired back. The way her voice settled on the *sir* made him think the designation wasn't meant as a compliment, but rather an insult.

He closed the gap between them, seizing the top handle of her cracked Samsonite, swinging it beside his truck as he bit his tongue. "Look like a rancher? What does a rancher even look like?" He muttered it under his breath, but loud enough for her to hear.

In all honesty, he figured he did in fact look exactly as one would imagine a rancher to look. Skin kissed by the sun in a perma-tan, hair worn long and the same uniform sported by all the men on his ranch—worn jeans and a flannel shirt topped with an oiled Stetson.

"I wouldn't dare to presume. And neither should you. Talk about judging a book by its cover—you're a proper chav, I'd say." She narrowed her eyes at him, the final pronouncement sounding more like a threat than an observation.

"You'll forgive my audacity," he replied. Her indignation was reassuring and he did his best to sound affable.

"Right. So it's sorted, then. I'm the tutor." Her cheeks colored as she added, "The *Oxford-educated* tutor, if you must."

"Yep, I must."

She tightened her lips again. "You're not allowed to park here. I've seen them yelling at people, even if it's only for a few minutes. We shouldn't dawdle." Mary hurried toward her bags, smiling politely. "I'll just grab the rest of my things."

He waved in the direction of the squat man doing a second drive-by in the parking enforcement vehicle. "Gus, nice to see you." Mary's smile froze in place as Gus waved back with a smile.

Better she learn sooner as opposed to later that he could park wherever he wanted in Bozeman. There was a different set of rules for a Hartmann.

She felt sucker punched. What had the director of the recruitment agency said? *This family is Montana royalty.* So, fancy, she expected. The spanking-new truck? *No surprise.* But things certainly were bigger in America, hot cowboy included. One look at Nick Hartmann and all the oxygen in her body escaped her. Yep, sucker punched. Tutoring was now the last thing on her mind.

He was tall and broad, living up to every girlhood

fantasy of an American cowboy she'd ever had, which, given the worn paperback romance collection she treasured, was quite a lot.

Longish dark hair was tied back and he wore a plaid shirt, the pattern at odds with the tailored fit. The way it stretched, snug across his chest, screamed expensive. Bespoke. High-end. The shirt tucked into a pair of jeans, blue-black in color, held in place with a wide leather belt. When his brown eyes made contact with hers, she wished for a brief moment she'd worn her own clothes instead of her sister's.

By any definition the man was breathtaking. *Word*taking, really. She swallowed. He was the best-looking man she'd ever seen in real life. And he was also her new employer. *Perfect.*

The beep from his key fob opened the flatbed and Nick heaved her second bag up into the back with ease. He hadn't struggled in the least, swinging the hefty luggage as though it were a bag of crisps and not a twenty-three-kilo rucksack. He turned, bumping into her.

"Oof," she let out as her body pressed into him. "I p-packed all my books in my carry-on so they wouldn't charge me an overweight fee," she stammered. She blushed at his proximity and felt a wave of heat rush to her cheeks.

He smiled. "I've gotta admit, I'm not sure what the going rate is for a checked bag these days." Nick straightened but didn't step away. His eyes studied her and she got the distinct impression he hadn't quite made up his mind about her yet.

She was standing close to him. Closer than she'd intended, and with the realization she had crossed some sort of invisible line, she stepped back and looked up. Fingers nervously tucked a loose wisp of hair behind her ear, and she backed away a few more paces before spinning and opening up the passenger door, stepping up into the truck.

Her buckle clicked into place, the safety belt fastened securely by the time he assumed the driver's seat. Her finger tapped a staccato beat on her thigh and she stared wide-eyed at the inside of the truck. This would all be easier if he was less attractive. A little less like every cowboy fantasy she'd dreamed up and a little more like a man she could shrug away. Because men like him were dangerous, and she was not in a position to let anyone in. More importantly, she was not in a position to fail.

Nick seemed to drive the forty miles to the ranch on autopilot, replacing one hand on the steering wheel with a knee. Opening his shoulder in her direction he turned and asked, "How was your flight?"

"Which one?" She smiled, but then added, "The trip was lovely. Long, bloody tiring, but lovely." Great. If there were to be more questions, she hoped they were all this surface level.

"Yep. That transatlantic will get you."

"I guess now I know." With his eyes now on the road, she could study him, overt in her curiosity. His jaw was square and strong, the shadow of a full beard on his chin. She felt a chill despite the strong sun and wondered if perhaps she was feeling the side effects of what she'd done sinking in. Or maybe she was feeling anxiety. Her cousin might have been right about this plan being a terrible idea. She bit her lip, savoring the quick jolt of ensuing pain.

"Alix has been here a few days. She's having quite the time settling in." The muscle along his jaw tightened as he swallowed, the marvelous Adam's apple bobbing with the action.

"Sure. Well, it's all been rather fast, hasn't it?" She twisted her fingers in her lap, pulling at a knuckle until it clicked with a satisfying pop.

"Fast is one way to put it."

Looking out the window at the vast expanse of fields, she squinted at the cattle spread far into the distance. Cattle, horses and a chance to heal. For her and for Alix. She needed to focus on the girl and her own new role as Mary "Poppins" Kelly. Alix was the reason she'd come. Alix, and the letter in her purse. The promise she hadn't made to her sister, but one she intended to keep. This contract was her chance to make it up to the universe and add a much-needed deposit in her karmic bank. Not that she believed in karma. It hardly seemed a good idea to believe in something that could serve her an epic bill.

"Sure. Yes. It's been a tough week." Nick broke the quiet with his observation. She looked at the thin watch on her wrist, also formerly her sister's. Within a quarter of an hour, they should arrive at the ranch, if her research was at all accurate. Research had never been a strong suit.

So what if she was impersonating her sister, taking

this tutoring gig in her stead? If she did a bad thing for a good reason, she was fairly sure it was okay.

For now, Rose Kelly stared out the window, forcing her stomach to stop twisting with every ounce of will-power she possessed as they drove toward the Yellow-stone River. Toward the Beartooth Mountains. Toward a plan to make it better. Or at least to make it okay.

Rose swallowed and fought back the tears that had threatened to fall ever since her sister had died. It wasn't fair. Mary was the good girl, and Rose the wild child.

Now, Rose had one chance to make a difference, to fulfill her sister's dream and pay an appropriate tribute to the person who had raised her. Perhaps accepting a private tutoring gig only to donate the lion's share of the proceeds to blind kids in India might not have been the way she'd thought she'd spend the next six months, but to Mary? The charity was everything. And with Mary gone? Rose was going to make sure every kid Mary had promised surgery would get it. And helping a newly or-phaned sixteen-year-old? Rose might not be an Oxford-educated tutor, but she was uniquely experienced and qualified to help an orphaned girl like Alix. No one could know better what it felt like to be alone at sixteen, and Rose was still rocking her own brand of grief, fresh and smarting at the mere thought of her sister.

If she could do something, anything, to make Mary's life goals happen, she was going to give it her honest best effort. Even if it meant signing her sister's name on a tutoring contract, and flying across the ocean in her stead to homeschool the closest thing to ranching royalty America had. If karma had a bill to settle, it would have to find Rose in Montana.

Two

Ben was waiting for him on Pax, the dark bay gelding he'd purchased earlier in the season, at 11:55 a.m., as agreed. Rowen, Nick's stallion, was saddled and stamping by his side. His best friend didn't say anything; instead, he tilted a cold bottle of beer in Nick's direction from atop his horse. "You're late," he accused.

Ben's dark hair was tucked behind his ears, and his beard had grown in. His bachelor status? Incorrigible. He was good-looking enough to require no effort to meet women, and the less he tried, the more he succeeded. It was an enviable quality.

"I asked Gary to saddle him up," Ben called down from Pax, nodding toward Rowen.

"Presumptuous of you. Forgive my tardiness, I've had quite the day." Nick smiled, ducking his head so the brim of his hat shielded his face. Ben had been a friend long enough to read a tight lip and, as a fellow rancher, could likely deduce precisely the distress it kept at bay.

"It's not even noon," was all Nick could think to say to the proffered beer as he slipped the toe of a boot into the stirrup.

"It's noon somewhere," Ben assured, and Nick accepted the drink with a matching grin. "Yer mom called," he added.

Nick assumed as much. Josephine Hartmann was a formidable force of nature, and, as the lawyer had informed him, executor of Austin's estate. Frankly, he was surprised she hadn't been nominated with the guardianship as well, although he hadn't ruled out the possibility she'd nominate herself in the aftermath. "Yep, I imagine she did."

Nick's phone blinked with six missed calls from Jo, but he wasn't ready to return them just yet. He exhaled and took a deep swig from the cold bottle. He needed more than a pilsner to face his mother. He needed time.

The two men cantered through an open field without the crushing pressure to fill each static moment with chatter, the hard-earned product of their thirty-year friendship.

"So Josephine told me about Alix. Hilarious. You're saddled with a kid, after all you've done to avoid 'em."

Nick turned a slanted brown eye in Ben's direction, and offered a dry, "Hilarious," in answer.

"Jo said she's at boarding school at least?"

"*Was* at boarding school. She was expelled. She's here now."

Ben let out a low whistle. "Sounds like this Alix sure is your niece, after all. Looks like you've got yourself a hell-raiser."

"Perfect, it should make running the ranch loads easier." Nick rolled his eyes.

"Didn't realize you and Austin were talking?"

Nick kept his eyes on the horizon and clucked at Rowen. "We weren't," he answered simply.

"But you're his daughter's guardian? That doesn't make sense."

"Yeah, well, that's Austin for you. Smarter than all of us, just ask him." Nick immediately regretted the sharp retort. He couldn't ask him. Austin was dead.

"You're still mad, then?"

"Why would I be mad? He and Katherine are—were—perfect for each other. I should have thanked him for chewing my leg outta that bear trap."

"Hardly the way to refer to your ex-girlfriend."

"I think the statute of limitations on ex-girlfriends expires after fifteen years."

"I didn't realize you were the forgiving type."

"I'm not. Neither was he. This…this…" Nick sputtered, turning in the saddle to face his friend. "This is exactly like Austin. Make me guardian after I swore never to have kids. He finds a way to stick it to me even from beyond the grave. Well, fine. Bet he didn't think I'd use his daughter as the vote to change the tides on this ranch."

Ben said nothing; a rancher himself, he knew the weight of responsibility Nick shouldered. In Montana, the Kingsman plot was second only to the Hartmanns' in terms of size, and while Ben's family focused more on horses than cattle, their outfit dated back generations. The Kingsman family were the only ranch in riding distance, which meant the friendship between the two men spanned decades. They rode a few more minutes in easy silence as Nick veered toward the stream, sliding off moments later to water Rowen.

"So if you're her guardian, what does that mean about the sale?" Ben slid down from the bay, voice low, and he spoke without making eye contact. It was a tough scab to pick at, but the ranch was on both their minds. How could it not be? The fight had been looming for years, ever since Nick's mother ceded early access to his inheritance.

Nick didn't answer; instead, he drew the stub of his fingernail across the label of the now empty beer bottle. The sweating bottle had dampened the paper, and it peeled away easily. Now? As guardian to Alix, the sixteen-year-old sole heir to Austin's interest, all decisions relating to her share of the estate were *his* to make. Nick peeled back another chunk of label. He wasn't ready to admit, even to his best friend, that the first call he had made, moments after learning his brother had died in a helicopter accident, had been to their real estate broker to suspend the ranch listing.

"There are two years until she comes of age. For those two years, I'm not selling. Evie and Amelia can sit tight."

Ben nodded, unflappable in his support, despite having fostered a deep affection for the twins, one of Nick's sisters in particular. "Two years can go by awful fast, Nick," he warned.

Nick flexed the muscle in his jaw. He knew the race of the clock all too well. First and foremost in his mind? He didn't have long to make the kid fall in love with Montana, with their legacy. If he could get her to fall in love with the land, she'd never sell it. He grimaced as he thought of the facility with which the twins and Austin had insisted on that very action, but that was his father's fault, not the land's.

"She's going to love it here." He repeated the mantra he'd been uttering as a prayer all week.

"You're gonna do fine, buddy, don't sweat it." Ben winked at him.

"Might help if I knew anything about teenage girls?" Nick scratched again at his label, balling up the bits he'd removed and wadding them into a small ball, which he rolled between his fingers.

"I seem to remember you were popular back in the day?"

Taking careful aim, Nick flicked the damp wad in Ben's direction, making contact with his friend's Adam's apple. "I doubt it's going to be the same."

Ben rubbed his neck and eyed his friend. "Something tells me you're gonna do just fine, buddy. Come on." He hiked himself back up onto the horse, and Nick followed suit.

They rode in silence most of the way. Until Ben interrupted, voicing another concern.

"You given any thought as to how you're going to manage to make her love it here?" Ben finally offered.

"I'm not sure you're going to sell this place to a sixteen-year-old based on a forty-minute commute to the nearest high school."

"I'm not going to." Nick smiled, thanking the stars his plan didn't include a commute.

"Pretty sure school is compulsory, buddy." Ben raised an eyebrow and took another swig of beer as they trotted toward the horizon.

"Oh, she's going to do school. I hired Mary Poppins, or rather, I commissioned the lawyer to hire Mary Poppins. She goes by Mary Kelly."

"You're hiring your sixteen-year-old niece a governess? Can I be there when you tell your mom?"

Nick frowned. His friend had a point. His mother wasn't likely to be on board with the homeschooling idea. Thing was, Nick could barely remember a time he'd been doing what his mom approved of. But it was too late to turn back now. "Not a governess—well, sorta, I guess, but more of a private tutor. The tutor I hired is the recent valedictorian of the year, an Oxford grad."

"Oxford? As in England? Oh my." Ben lifted a hand to his forehead with dramatic flair.

"Alix's been kicked outta three boarding schools. According to Saul, I need the best." Nick shrugged. If the kid wanted to come home so bad, he'd see to it she never left.

"Is she hot?" Ben asked.

"I hope you're asking about the tutor, and I'll remind you she's now on my staff, but you're gonna find out soon enough to decide for yourself. She's already here, getting a rundown from Samantha." He slipped his empty into the saddlebag trailing from the rear horn of his saddle, grateful to have sidestepped the question of her appearance.

Yes. She was hot. More than hot. She was a tamale of trouble.

"Samantha? The assistant you kissed, then brushed off? Is that wise?" Ben asked. It was easy to forget his confidant knew about his past, but Ben never let him forget long.

"Samantha's capable, and there's nothing going on between us. Plus, she was the one who went over the contract with the lawyer. She's going over the Montana curricula and associated homeschooling expectations from the state. I'll meet with Mary when we get back. Her bags are still in the truck."

Ben said nothing and just raised his eyebrows. Any higher and they risked running into his hairline.

Riding with his best friend was cathartic. Ben didn't ask about Austin or Jackson. Heck, he didn't even ask about how Nick was feeling about all this. He didn't need to. They'd spent enough nights drinking and scheming together to know better.

Perhaps it was rash. Hiring a tutor, sight unseen and at top dollar nonetheless. But Alix Hartmann was home. The ranch he'd thought lost was saved, if only temporarily. Nick could suffer whatever consequences he needed to endure to keep Hartmann Estates and the ranch running. Even if it meant raising Austin and Katherine's love child as his own.

At least, for now, he had his horse, his friend and a second beer. "Cheers, buddy," he said. "And thanks."

Nick motioned for the chair in front of him. "Take a seat, won't you, Mary." He smiled at her. "Scotch?"

She arrived at the office moments after he'd stepped out of his quarters, freshly showered and ready for business. Mary closed the few feet between them and sank into the chair he motioned her toward, nodding.

"I suppose it's past midnight in London," he said. He rose, making his way to the discreet wet bar his father had installed. Four years since his dad died and it still felt like he was trespassing when he was in this office. The feeling caught him unawares when he least expected it. Nick kept the bar stocked, and as his fingers brushed the assorted bottles, they paused on the Johnnie Walker Black. Best get this conversation on the right track. Without turning to face her, he asked, "Ice?"

From the warmth in her scoff, he guessed at the smile accompanying her refusal. He determined perhaps she was more suited for Montana than he'd initially feared. Maybe Oxford, or the recruitment firm, did a good job with their screening process, after all.

"So why Montana?" he asked, handing her a glass. She studied the amber liquid, surprising him by dipping a finger into the Scotch and raising it to her lips. He stared as a small pink tongue flicked to lick an errant drip of whiskey before it dripped down her finger. He cleared his throat in an effort to clear his mind. It was not the time to be thinking about her tongue, as delectable as it might be.

"Why not Montana?" There was a flippancy to her tone, incongruent with his vision of a British nanny-turned-tutor. But that avenue of thought had proved difficult to defend earlier, so he pushed it back.

Roberta, his housekeeper, had set a fire, and it crackled satisfactorily in the wide fireplace behind them. He was struck with the realization that Mary still wore her coat. "Shall I take that for you?"

"Right, yes, sorry. After meeting with Samantha, I was exploring with Alix, and we lost track of the time." She blushed. Shifting in her chair, she shrugged off her coat, fishing one hand free at a time in an effort to avoid relinquishing her drink. He suppressed a smile.

Under her coat, poorly disguised by the cardigan, was the lush body, there for the admiring.

"She's lovely—Alix, I mean." Mary blushed.

Relieved of her outerwear, she fastened the loose button at the neck of her sweater and sat on her free hand. "I am sorry about your brother."

He grunted. It was the same song he'd heard all week. Strangers offering condolences as though they would offer a reprieve to the pain he'd shouldered every waking moment since the cursed phone call last week. Austin's death stirred up everything. The betrayal. The loss. The certainty he'd never be able to yell at him again, no matter how much he deserved it. There was one way to forget the pain, and another deep look at her lush body offered him every confidence it would be effective. Suddenly it was hard to think of anything else. He cleared his throat and answered on autopilot. "Yep, it was a surprise."

"The agency told me it was a helicopter accident." She took a sip of her drink and looked up at him.

Her eyes were pools of light blue fire. It was like looking at the center of a lit match. Similarly, he was sure if he held the gaze too long, he'd burn. She looked away first, suddenly deeply interested in the faceted glass he had poured for her.

"Yes, well, Austin always did like his helicopters." It was easier brushing off the mention of his brother rather than bringing them both down with the harsh realities of the recent deaths.

Her fingers tightened around the etched glass of her rock glass. "Private jet or nothing, that's what I say." She smiled in sarcasm and he surprised himself with a laugh in response.

"So Alix. She's in year eleven?" She raised an eyebrow…

He knew she had this information. He'd submitted answers to a barrage of questions prior to signing a contract with the agency that sent her, outlining all he knew, and highlighting a lot he didn't know about his niece. So why was she asking now? He studied her, eyes wide and open, and decided he didn't care why. Small talk had never been his forte, but so long as he wasn't doing the heavy lifting, it was fine.

"Yep. Pulled her from the boarding school. Well—" he rubbed at his chin "—I pulled her to avoid expulsion. She was caught drinking on campus, a serious no-no in the boarding school world." He took another sip, draining his glass. Hesitating only a moment, he uncorked the bottle to pour a refill. He motioned in her direction and she held her glass forward, though the bottom third of her drink was still there.

"I mean, who hasn't had a drink at boarding school, right?" she joked.

"I wouldn't have pegged you for the type, Oxford." He smiled as she reddened.

"I meant, given the circumstances." Her eyes flashed, and she pushed her shoulders back.

His desk was orderly, not a page out of place. All the files relating to his brother's estate, including his will and last wishes, were in the same stack. The Alix files were next. Three pens were spaced evenly beside the stacked files, and he picked up his favorite: a Mont Blanc fountain pen. Picking up the gift from his dad, he wiggled it on his fingers. "I don't want her to hate it here." *Sometimes when you don't know what to say you should start with the truth.*

"Well, I'll have to see how I can help with that, shall I?" She smiled and took another sip of Scotch.

He shook his head. Anything to break their gaze. He was staring again. "She's a good student, or at least it seems so." He pushed the file the headmistress had sent him across the table and Mary leaned forward. The lean offered a new angle to the view down her top and he felt his body tighten in appreciation.

"Right. Should make things easier. Of course, academics is just part of the high school experience, hardly the brilliant bit." She fidgeted on her chair, mouth screwed up in an adorable bow.

"What?" he asked because he had to know.

She pulled at a loose curl, straightening the hair to

her shoulder before letting it spring back. "Homeschooling seems a bit much, don't you think? I mean, wouldn't you be miffed to go from an upstate New York boarding school to a private tutor in the Montana wilderness?" She blushed again. "Not that I'm trying to talk myself out of a job—it can just help to have a little insight."

"I didn't think you were here to interview me?" He stood, placing his cup on the desk. Beads of sweat from the glass made their way down the side of the tumbler in protest to the heat. It was unseasonably hot for May, and the cozy fire wasn't helping. Neither was the fiery tutor.

"I didn't mean—" she started.

Nick bit the inside of his cheek. *He* hadn't meant to put her on guard. "Sorry. I, ah, haven't had a lot of time to process. I think what she needs now is family. To rediscover where she came from. It's complicated."

She shifted in her seat, nodding.

"Rather a long day, I'll show you to your quarters." He moved toward the door, and she stood and followed. The last thing he wanted to do was talk about the reasons he needed Alix to love the ranch, or the drama around all things Katherine.

What began as a *how do you do* had disintegrated quickly. She followed the cowboy, as she referred to him mentally since accepting the position, out of his office.

He didn't speak as he led them through the home. *Home* felt an inadequate description for the ranch palace he—rather they—lived in. Soaring high ceilings met walls of windows offering incredible views of the Beartooth Mountain range. Polished logs paired with brass light fixtures created a rustic-chic ambience and she was overwhelmed, not for the first time since her arrival, with the feeling of being small. Everything in this ranch was oversize. The polished leather couches spanned seven feet, and were overstuffed, draped in skins and furs.

"Is that real?" She wished her voice was louder.

Nick, not pausing his stride, spoke over his shoulder. "What? The antelope?" He nodded toward a mounted head. In another setting, it would look rough, but here, surrounded by opulence, it was wild. "Yeah, we've got big-game hunting on the ranch—got that one when I was fifteen. My first buck. Dad had it mounted."

She took two paces to match each one of his long strides, and she hopped to keep up with him, not wanting to miss the tail end of his anecdotes. *A hunter?* A primal desire sparked in her stomach, but she squeezed her fingers into her palm, allowing the nails to dig into the flesh of her hand. She wasn't here for that.

He led her up a wide staircase to a second-floor hallway, lit with several skylights. The third door on the left opened into a large bedroom with windows overlooking a field of waist-high grasses. In the distance, she saw cattle grazing. In juxtaposition to the wildness of the setting, her room was the picture of opulence. A four-poster bed, with four extralarge pillows and a fluffy duvet covered in a stitched quilt. The room also had its own fireplace, which housed another cheery, blazing fire. Muslin drapes framed the picture windows, which overlooked an expanse of the most beautiful rugged countryside she'd ever seen.

"Your room," he said.

She sucked in a breath. It was a far cry from her tiny flat in London. Her cousin had been delighted to sub-lease it from her, even on a moment's notice, qualifying her flat as a "huge space." She doubted she'd refer to any part of England as huge ever again after this experience.

"Thanks, it's lovely. The room. The… Everything." She stumbled on the words. A small part of her felt a pang of niggling guilt for her ruse. It was harder than she expected, pretending to be her sister, but a quick, deep breath renewed her confidence in her decision. She would help Alix, and this family. There was nothing wrong about bloody well enjoying herself in the process. She believed with all her soul there was no one better suited to help a sixteen-year-old orphan than herself.

Her luggage was waiting in the far corner of her room. Nick paused in the doorway, shoulder propped against the frame, studying her.

"Quite the view," she said softly, and she heard the invitation in her own voice. *Maybe he'll stay awhile.* Although the thought was nerve-racking.

"Yep."

His one-word answers were infuriating. She cast a glance back in his direction, wondering, not for the first time, if he was biting back what he really thought.

She turned to face him, and sat on the edge of the large bed, sinking into a duvet of soft feathers. A smile spread across her face. "This is the most comfortable bed I've ever had."

"Yep. I, ah… I'll see you for dinner? Down the stairs

to the left of the entrance. The cook made up a spread
for us. We tend to eat at six. You'll join us?"

Us was likely him and Alix, but she was still stum-
bling on the first bit of his pronouncement. "Cook?"

"We have an independent staff to tend to the home.
I'll introduce you tomorrow. The estate is parceled into
different acreages—a hospitality and hotel branch on
the east end of the lot, a fishing retreat closer to Bill-
ings. We're in the cattle end here, with our offices for
the Hartmann Corp headquartered in the east wing of
the home." He gestured toward a cluster of buildings
set at a distance near a clearing. She nodded.

"It's a working ranch here, see?" He entered her room
and walked toward the window, setting both large hands
on the sill, nodding toward the fields to the west. "Hartmann Homestead is just shy of two hundred thousand
acres. We also have a few fields planted and thirty thousand acres of waterfront to the Yellowstone."

His shoulders relaxed, and she stared at his shirt,
tucked into another pair of dark jeans, hugging his
thighs just enough to make her sweat a little.

"I could take you girls out tomorrow? On an expe-
dition to see the grounds? Get you both on horses?" He
turned and smiled. A welcome change from his ever-
present tight-lipped frown.

She found herself at a loss for words, nodding dumbly.
How would she keep up the ruse of being her proper sister if she saw this man on a horse? It was hard to imagine
her attraction could burn any brighter, but an adolescent
chaperone seemed a good idea. She leaned back, the wall

by her door serving as adequate support for her weak-kneed reaction to the proposal.

"Right, then. See you shortly." He turned and headed toward the door. His arm brushed against her as he shimmied past, lighting her blood on fire.

The good thing about his departure was the opportunity it presented to watch him walk away. The man was delicious. Mary would have had a heart attack. Rose choked back the thought. The levity offered through her attraction was an effective reprieve from the constant guilt she carried around, but with him gone, the guilt was back. Mary couldn't have had a heart attack. Not after Rose had been responsible for her death.

Her hand slipped to her pocket and her fingers traced across the cool comfort of the phone. Clunky, serviceable and not hers.

It was past five thirty, so not yet midnight. She dialed her cousin.

Tapping the back of Mary's phone, her finger became a staccato metronome.

"Jeez, Rose, it's nearly midnight," Ellen answered, adding mumbled curses to the greeting.

Rose fell back onto the feather bed and pressed the phone to her ear. "Right. Sorry to wake you, then." She fought a wave of exhaustion threatening to overpower her.

"Are you coming home?" The question echoed through the phone, and Rose felt a surge of annoyance.

"Home? I thought you got it, Ellen. This is home for me now. I'm finishing this. I accepted the contract, the post, for Mary, and I'll not quit."

"You're impersonating your dead sister for your dead sister?" Ellen's tone was imbued with disapproval.

"You know why I'm doing this." Rose sighed.

"Tell me you're not doing this because of *them*?"

"Mary pledged to help, and I'll be damned if I have to write the organization and say the money isn't coming, after all."

"I'm sure they'd understand." The exasperation was gone from her tone, and Ellen sounded small and very far away.

"No. I can't say it. I can't tell them."

"Tell them…?"

"That she's gone." Rose swallowed. *Gone* was a nice word for dead, but she doubted it would provide any relief for the association her sister had volunteered with over the past decade. Mary had been so excited when she was crowned valedictorian. She knew then she'd get a contract like this, and had been so confident she'd pledged to pay for the children's surgeries before signing with a family. Twenty-seven kids she'd agreed to sponsor. *Overachiever.*

Rose scratched the nail polish chipping off her thumb. Funny thing was, a contract like this *was* enough money. She could correct the vision for twenty-seven nearly blind kids in India. Rose wasn't about to call them and say, *Sorry, the wrong sister died so you kids are plumb outta luck.* When the contract fell in her lap, she'd accepted without thinking. Now? She could fund her sister's legacy. And the best part? The job was also helping a kid.

"She's an orphan, Ellen. A sixteen-year-old orphan.

No one is gonna understand this kid better than I can." Tap, tap, tap…the finger's speed increased against the phone, a thriving pulse to her temper.

"The idea wasn't to uphold the pledge at any cost. Mary trained for years for her teaching degree."

"I know," Rose snapped back. "I shared a room with her the whole time. Who do you think helped with the cue cards for her to study? Who helped prep for the exams—"

"Who never missed a student party?"

A lump formed in her throat, and she knew from her grieving in the past month that the lump wouldn't dislodge without a good cry. It was something she was ill-prepared to do on the phone, let alone twenty minutes before dinner with Cowboy and Alix. She sighed. "What's this really about, Ellen? You think I can't do it or I won't do it well enough? Or is it that you're jealous?" Perhaps the last was a low blow but she was too tired to care.

"I don't know what would give you the impression I'm jealous—"

"Alix only has a few months left of the school year and if I manage to help her through it *everybody wins*. Even the SightSavers. I might not be tutor of the year, but it's year eleven, not neurosurgery. Plus, if I pull this off, no one has to call and cancel anything. I can be there for Alix, pay for those poor kids to have surgery and make a difference. I can finish what Mary started. I owe her that."

She heard her cousin's exhale through the phone. "Right."

"Look, you're not going to change my mind. You couldn't in England and you won't now. Anyway, I doubt there's a soul on earth more qualified to mentor a newly orphaned sixteen-year-old girl." Rose swore under her breath. She didn't need a teaching degree to help. And she didn't need a designer dress to sleep with the god of ranchers. Girl's gotta take the edge off somehow, and it was important that in pretending to be her sister she didn't lose herself. With Mary gone, she was her own conscience now.

She blushed. Sleeping with the rancher? The thought had come from nowhere, unbidden, or had it come from the stubborn spark lit in the airport? She supposed it didn't matter. Spark or not, she was not going to lean into the fire. She was here for her sister's legacy. She was here to help Alix. She was *not* going to fall for a cowboy, no matter how much she wanted to.

Three

"It's good to see you, kid." Nick stood in the doorframe of the room designated for Alix, wondering at the truth in his statement. The girl was on her bed, earphones in, back turned to him, and it was good to see her.

No answer. *Okay, not unusual for a teenager, right?* He wasn't going to express his sympathies. He knew from the past week that it was more irritating than comforting.

"I hope it's not weird. Being here, I mean." He stepped into the room and made his way over to the bed, the setting sun casting his dark shadow on her quilt. The girl looked up and Nick shuddered. She had been crying. Not his forte.

"Why would it be weird? 'Cause I don't know you? Literally, never met you in my life, and now you're my guardian or whatever?" Her eyes sparkled as she spat her answer at him. She was right, but still… He glanced at his hands, wondering what he had done to wave red at this adolescent. He had angered the bull. No clean way around this arena.

"I meant due to the fact that I wasn't here when you met Mary, er, Ms. Kelly." He shifted his weight from foot to foot. *Yep, I shoulda handled the introduction myself. Rookie mistake.*

"Whatever. I'm too old for Mary *bloody* Poppins, anyway." She laced the superlative with a mock accent and he stiffened at her tone.

"She's not a governess, if that's what you're thinking. I just figured you wouldn't want to take the bus to school." His weight faced back onto his left leg, and his hip cocked forward, nervous stance in place.

"Bus? What makes you think I'd take the bus? Isn't the one silver lining in all this that I can now afford a car for myself?" Her voice caught on the last word and Nick fought the impulse to give her a hug.

"Let's start with a good report card, shall we? I tend not to issue car keys following an expulsion, which I'm sure you can agree is reasonable." He shifted his weight from foot to foot. *Do it, Nick. Sit on the bed.* He gave in to his inner voice and sat on the edge of the bed.

"Whatever. Fine. It's fine. I'll be fine. It's all fine." She picked up her phone and jabbed at the screen, a rude dismissal, but forgivable.

"Really, kid. It's a tough hand. But I'm your uncle. This place is as much yours as mine, and I'm hoping you can find a way to make it your home." He spoke in a measured pace, calm and quiet, the way he would talk to a horse he needed to break. "When things got bad for me, the mountains, this land—" He pinked. "I mean, the land can heal you."

"Didn't think it could get too bad for the golden boy," she sniffed.

Austin had called him golden boy. Just the one time, but it had been enough. Maybe she didn't know. What her mom had done? Well, it wasn't his place to say. Not now, anyway. He cleared his throat. "Golden boy, am I now? I guess I can understand how your dad might have thought that." He swallowed, not sure how he could unpack the fight that had led to Austin's departure, and the slur that had followed. "You can just call me uncle. Or Nick."

"Whatever."

"I guess the land means something different to everyone. Maybe just find out what it means to you?"

"Sure. Not like I have a choice now, do I?" Her chin jutted forward and, for a moment, she looked twelve and not sixteen, large eyes wide and fringed with heavy lashes. The picture of Katherine.

"Dinner's at six. Dining room is the last door on the left." He turned. Best not to force things too fast.

"I'm not hungry." Despite the show of turning up the volume, she answered immediately.

"We eat as a family." Again, like a horse, he needed to show who held the reins.

He interpreted the eye roll as tacit agreement.

"So we're family now?"

"You can't choose your kin, Alix." He kept his tone consistent.

"You're telling me," she sighed.

He stiffened and, in a fluent movement, stood up from the bed.

"I didn't mean you," she added, her quiet voice stopping him in his tracks. "I mean, it's alright being here, I guess."

"Don't worry about it." He turned and looked at her. "It can only get easier from here."

He turned and left, pausing only a moment to cast a glance over his shoulder. Kid was nodding her head to the beat of whatever she was listening to. Angry, sure.

Hell, he deserved it.

Rose applied a fresh coat of lipstick and whipped a brush through her curls, jutting a quick glance at her reflection. The brush did little to tame her curls, although her look was much improved after a quick smear of hair defrizzer serum from a bottle whose packaging she quickly concluded oversold the effects but smelled good. She had on a fresh top—a simple white button-up that hugged her figure—and a new pair of blue jeans. Retrieving her heeled ankle boots, she slipped them on. She would now be three inches closer to the mouth that had driven her to distraction. Yes, it was quite a problem. She was looking for a distraction.

Without the anchor of the good angel on her shoulder, the older sister who kept her conscience, Rose felt a spell of indecision about whether or not she should pursue that distraction.

Poking her head out of her bedroom, she retraced the path to her new room, pausing at the head of the double-wide staircase. The creaking plank flooring throughout the home was double-glazed with a varnish so shiny she could make out her reflection in the polished wood-work. She smiled at it.

The dining room was easy to find. She followed her nose, and arrived at a Norman Rockwell painting. The table was heavily set with all the trimmings of what could have been an American Thanksgiving dinner, even though it was only May. Nick sat at the head of the table, with a sullen Alix to his right.

"This is quite something." Rose breezed into the dining room and took the vacant seat to Nick's left. The smells of roast turkey were mouthwatering, and the bird before them boasted a crackling brown glaze, triggering a roil of anticipation in her stomach.

"Some might say people were trying too hard." Alix did her best to sound disinterested, but Rose noticed a surreptitious swallow. It would be tough not to be affected by such a lovely dinner and the effort spent preparing it.

"Some others might find their manners and be grateful to have such a delicious meal waiting for them," Nick answered. He'd slid into the parental role with a facility that provoked the question of why such a handsome man as he didn't have kids and family of his own. *A man of mystery indeed.*

Classic teenage eye rolls answered, and Nick distributed a thick slab of turkey breast to Alix's plate, suggesting, "Try the cranberry sauce—they're from our own patch."

Rose, not to be put off by adolescent tension, helped herself to a turkey leg and all the fixings. She hadn't eaten since morning and was famished. Nick passed her the bowl of gravy, and his fingers brushed against hers. She bit her lip and looked away.

"This is lovely." She smiled, nodding at the offered wine bottle tipping toward her glass.

"Yep," the cowboy answered.

"So, Alix, I was thinking we could get a start tomorrow?" Rose busied herself slicing the meat off her turkey leg into even pieces on her plate, hoping her casual question would provoke some enthusiasm. The plan she'd conceived on the plane was to treat the adolescent the way she treated men she wanted to seduce—using nonchalance to draw them in. Be hard to get. Sitting in front of Alix now, Rose worried the idea was half-baked, but in for a penny, in for a pound. Plus, nonchalance was pretty much the only tool in her arsenal.

"If I have to." Alix shrugged.

"You have to," Nick confirmed. His tone gave no room for negotiation.

"Fine, then." She pushed her plate away from her. "I'm not hungry." She sulked as she moved away from the table.

"Alix?" Nick called. The girl didn't stop.

"That's teenagers for you, sangfroid the moment you suggest an early start," Rose remarked, before popping another slice of turkey onto her plate. The food was spectacular.

Nick tightened his mouth.

A toque blanche poked around the corner of the entrance and a small French chef arrived, balancing a plate of asparagus swimming in a yellow dressing.

"Mr. Hartmann, *voilà le plat du jour.*" He presented the platter with a flourish.

"Thanks, Pierre," Nick said. "Did you take a plate to Amelia?"

Her stomach tightened. *Who was Amelia?*

"No, sir, she's at the Stateman house this evening. It's just *vous trois…*er, *vous deux.*" The chef reddened.

"Sure, thanks."

"Enjoy your meal, mademoiselle." Pierre smiled and touched his hat in farewell. "The asparagus is perfection." He raised his fingers to his lips for a classic chef's kiss and left.

Nick refilled his wineglass, slamming the bottle back on the table without offering to refill hers. Just as well, it was still half-full. She took another sip and placed the glass back down loud enough to provoke his interest.

"Sorry, Oxford." He smiled at her, but his eyes were not focused. With his right hand, he spaced the cutlery before him evenly, three forks lined up from smallest to largest where they met his plate. He pushed his water glass out to align at a right angle.

"You have something against scalene triangles?" She laughed, pleased with herself. She'd been reading an idiot's guide to geometry on the plane and was pleased to work in some tutoring terminology. The opportunity to tease the cowboy was an unexpected bonus.

Nick swept the three forks together with the back of

his hand and shook his head. "Sometimes I like to organize things so they have a place."

She pushed her wineglass to a ninety-degree angle to her plate. "If I play by your rules, will you be nice to me?" She tilted her wineglass toward the bottle and smiled again.

His eyes flickered from her glass to her mouth, precisely the reaction she'd hoped for. Day one was coming to a close—it had to be well past two a.m. her time now—and she was tired. Too tired to keep up the charade of being her sister, of being good, and just tired enough to be deliciously herself.

He filled her glass and pushed his shoulders back into his chair. "To geometry."

"I've always preferred chemistry." The words escaped before she could stop them.

The line of muscle along his jaw flexed and he lifted his glass toward her. The dining room was so quiet she could hear her own pulse as she touched her glass to his with an exaggerated, "Cheers."

Chemistry indeed.

Four

One good thing about traveling from England to Montana was the time difference. It worked in her favor, and for once in her life, Rose was up before the sun. She was dressed before the snooze button, hit by habit, had shrieked.

Force of routine had her leaning toward a mirror putting on a quick coat of makeup and running a brush through her curls before she gave up trying to be fancy. She wanted to explore her surroundings and find a calm spot to think before her teaching duties began.

She'd stared at the ceiling for nearly an hour last night, eyes wide despite a heavy fatigue. Rose didn't want to be thinking about him. Blue jeans and cowboy boots, paired with a strong jaw and dimpled chin? Any woman in her right mind would be a little distracted, but she was going to be more like Mary. Behave in a way that would keep her sister close. It was the thoughts of her sister that stung, and finally sleep became a welcome escape from grief, sexy cowboy notwithstanding.

The front door to the ranch was eight feet across, but surprisingly light. She pulled it open and was grateful to see the hinges were recently greased. The door opened without a sound and two steps later she was in the great Montana outdoors.

From the window of her bedroom, she could spot the beginnings of a river, which was where she was headed. Her first step was to circle the home, so she turned left and rounded the manor.

The walls of the ranch were cut from large boulders of fieldstone in varying shades of gray. The stone foundation gave way to huge logs, hewn together with masterful carpentry. Never in her life had she seen such a sumptuous private residence, and the five minutes she'd allotted to round the home quickly turned into twenty. As she turned the corner of the front of the house, she discovered a second wing. This one featured floor-to-ceiling windows on the back side. She scurried past, grateful none of the main floor windows were lit at such an early hour.

The grass was wet with dew and the leather of her boots darkened at the damp licks of weeds and wildflowers. She didn't know what she was looking for per se, but was reasonably sure she'd know it when she found it. A wooden fence blocked the path, but it was made up of two logs, more to keep in cattle and horses than deter human passersby. She hiked a leg up and swung herself over. The fence had been visible from her window and she judged herself to be roughly halfway to her destination. Having cleared the fence, she pulled the phone from her pocket and dialed the voice mail.

"You've reached the voice mail of Mary Kelly. I'm terribly sorry but I seemed to have missed your call. Leave me your details and I will call you back as soon as I'm able. Cheerio." Her sister's voice was vibrant. The mix of proper and prim in her inflection firmly designated her as the good sister, as it had since childhood. Rose disconnected and redialed, listening again to her sister's voice. The words became the tone she marched to. You've reached, *two steps*, the voice mail, *three more steps*, of Mary Kelly, *three steps*. A step for each syllable, and by the third chorus she had arrived at the edge of a wood.

The gray moment before the sun rose had arrived and was breathtaking. Rose parked herself on the large rock, larger still than she had imagined from her window. Amazing how perspective could change so much. She sat on the rock and listened for the rushing of water, audible over the faint hum of her phone.

She was alone. It was breathtaking, beautiful and a massive challenge. She finally had a moment to cry. A moment to fall apart. She set an alarm on her phone. Five minutes. She was allowing herself five minutes to let go.

Putting the voice mail on speaker, she allowed her head to sink into her hands as she heard the ring of her sister's voice without having to hold the phone. It was the opposite of a selfie.

"You said you'd never leave me," she whispered. Her voice echoed with a hollow quality, reverberating off the damp air. Hearing it, she cried harder.

"You said you'd always be there for me!" she shouted this time, but fought the urge to hurl the phone away. Kicking the base of a tree, she fell back onto the ground, rubbing her toe.

Her phone alarm sounded. The five minutes felt both impossibly long and terribly short. No matter. The falling apart had to end now. She stood. The stream was nearby and splashing some cold water on her face seemed a good idea.

The creek proved easier to find than she anticipated, though it was another twenty minutes by foot from her rock. The rushing water was cold, but it wasn't the temperature that stilled her. Someone had proved an earlier riser than she, arriving before her.

He was a merman. Lithe and athletic, with not a spare ounce on him. "My word," she muttered under her breath. He looked precisely as she'd imagined. *Maybe better.*

Like a deer, frozen, she stood still. Nick was swimming in the punishingly cold creek. He got out of the water and she inhaled sharply. The man had the body of a marble statue. Even from her distance, she could count the ridges of muscle in his six—no, eight—pack. She swallowed. His arms. They had looked good in the plaid shirts she quickly discovered to be his uniform, but naked before her? She blushed. His swimsuit left not much to the imagination. The few gaps she needed to fill in herself she did with relish.

She backed up, stepping on a twig in the process. Because that's what happens to city slickers with leaden feet. They humiliate themselves in front of glorious mountain men.

"Mary? Is that you?" He was slipping on his clothes with depressing efficiency, and she quickened her pace.

"I'm just… I was just walking." Her voice carried a trace of her earlier lamenting, and she tried not to regret the crying.

Nick's agility allowed him to reclothe faster than Rose would have liked, and moments later he pulled on a shirt, fastening it as he walked toward her. "You found my swimming hole," he said as he walked, breath still short from the cold of the creek.

"I did. Not that it was hiding much. I can just see it from my window."

"I guess so." A worn towel was slung over his shoulder. Hardly the tool of such a wealthy man, but he proved down to earth, at least in private.

"You're up early." She'd mastered small talk from her stint working at a bar. A good way to avoid personal questions was to launch your own barrage of inquiry.

"Yep." His wet swimsuit radiated cold. The hair on her arms stood on end, from the cold. *Right*.

"I'm still juggling jet lag." It seemed as reasonable an excuse as any to be wandering the estate at five a.m.

Nick grunted, then turned his head in her direction. "Did you want to try a swim? I've been starting my day in this creek since I was just a kid."

Now that he had left the creek, a frigid swim held less appeal. "Maybe tomorrow?"

* * *

At first, he'd thought he was seeing a ghost. Suddenly he was fifteen, sneaking to meet his sweetheart for a predawn swim. He choked back surprise and swam toward the creek's edge, seeking comfort in the apparition.

He stopped a few feet from shore. He was sick of talking to ghosts. They were everywhere now. His dad. His brother. Katherine. The haunted face of his niece. Even the new tutor had an ache to her aura—not that he believed in auras.

The figure backed up, and a blond curl bounced with the momentum of her retreat. *Mary? Have you come to haunt me now, too?*

He paused in the water and rubbed his eyes. It *was* her. He smiled, relieved. She looked nothing like Katherine; maybe it was one of the things he liked about her. She looked sad, and Katherine hadn't wasted a moment of her life on that emotion.

Her second day on the ranch and she'd found him first thing. Temptation followed him, and he was feeling weaker by the instant. He wanted to forget all those ghosts, and the surefire way to do so was the only thing he could think about. She was dressed in a white T-shirt. Simple. Tight. A red bra visible through thin cotton. His brain, totally occupied with the fantasy of her dressed in only said red bra, was capable of only one-word answers in response to her chatter. It was the grief, he reasoned, that fueled his one-track mind.

He did have the presence of mind to suggest a predawn swim. He'd issued the invitation before he could stop the words. It was a terrible idea to see her in a swimsuit. Terrible and wonderful, an excruciating test of will.

"Maybe tomorrow," she said.

They walked the next few minutes in silence. Her face had a puffy quality to it, and her eyes had the tell-tale "too bright" sheen of having just poured buckets of tears.

He wasn't going to ask. It wasn't his business.

"Did you still want to go on that horse ride today?" Her voice was tentative as she focused on the trail before them, dancing around the larger rocks in the path.

Their ride over the property was the first step in his plan to get Alix to fall in love with the ranch. Show her the land. Getting to spend time with the perky tutor was just a bonus.

"We could. Sure."

She looked up at him, and in the momentary lapse of concentration, she stumbled on the rock with an anguished, "Ow, bollocks!"

He reared like a stallion. Mary was clutching her ankle. Not crying, a good sign as there were few things as frightening to Nick Hartmann as the sight of a weeping woman. "Are you okay?" The question felt redundant given her exclamation, but he couldn't stop himself.

"I've just twisted my ankle, but I'm sure it's fine." She reached her hand up toward his searchingly.

The small hand was cold and miniature in his own, and he gripped it as he pulled her to her feet. Mary leaned into his frame as they walked toward the ranch together. Her hip pressed into his side and all he could feel was her body against his. It was electric.

For a long while now, Nick had drawn a line around himself. A wall made of several unmovable bricks. Boss. Rancher. Son. He was the responsible one. It was a line no one crossed without asking. But here she was, pressed against him, in his space, crashing through his wall.

It felt good.

"Is this okay?" His arm snaked around her, pulling her against him, his body the support for each alternating step.

"Yes," she said through gritted teeth. Her face was drawn and white, freckles more visible against her blanched skin. He hadn't noticed the freckles until just then and was utterly charmed by them.

"We're not far," were the only words of comfort he could think of. She shifted, and he felt an arm twist around his waist, gripping his hip.

"I think I can make it if you help me."

"Sure. It's what I'm here for." And they sauntered forward. It was slow going, picking the way around ruts in the path. To her credit, she didn't complain, but following a lurch to cross a fallen log, she cursed.

"They teach you how to talk like that at Oxford?"

She paled. "No, but I moonlit as a barmaid. I've heard a lot worse, as I'm sure you have."

He smiled at the pinch he received to his side. "Indeed. Careful, Oxford, I'm playing nice." He swallowed. It was too soon to joke. Regardless of her starring role in his dreams last night, pleasantries were still in order.

She was his employee. He wasn't about to start anything with the hired help. Not again.

Blushing vermilion, her eyes stood out a shocking blue, two cobalt gems flashing at him. "Ever think I've been playing nice, too?"

"Nice or not, I don't see how you're going to limp back to the house. We've got a half mile ahead of us." That was valid. What he didn't say was just as true— namely, he wanted to hold her.

She grimaced. "I'm doing okay."

"I wasn't saying otherwise, just that we'll be an hour getting back at this rate."

"I'm not sure what you're suggesting? Not likely I'll finish the sprint if that's what you had in mind?"

"Not exactly. I was thinking I could carry you. It'd be faster, and I need to meet the men at six thirty."

"Carry me? A half mile? No. You just go ahead. I'll find a stick or something and limp at my own pace. I don't want to keep you." She was blabbering, perhaps due to her own susceptibility to their chemistry, and it was charming.

"If you think I'm leaving you to struggle with a stick, you've got another think coming." He bent and, before she could object, scooped an arm behind her knees, pulling them out from under her. She fell back in the shallow of his arms. "Much better," he confirmed, picking up the pace with a dogged saunter back to the house.

She didn't say anything, but after a few strides her head settled into the nook of his shoulder. Maybe he shouldn't admit that the fit of her, against his chest, was validating. Her hair, the wild curls soft against the hollow of his neck, smelled like lavender and soap, a clean, fresh smell tempting him to close his eyes and lose himself in her femininity.

Mary was hot against his chilled skin, and he was aware of every inch of her pressed against his. Nick swallowed, renewing a concerted effort not to notice the feel of her body in his arms. How easily he'd lifted her, the slack in her neck as she fell against him. The weight of a woman relaxed in his grasp.

Too soon, they arrived. He hesitated only a moment before nudging the side door open with his shoulder and continuing inside.

"I'm sure I can make it the last few steps."

"I'm your employer, and I'm insisting on a safe delivery." A weak argument, sure, but he wasn't ready to put her down.

Her answer was to settle back, soft in his arms.

Making quick work of the stairs, he brought her up to her room where he hesitated.

"Thanks," she sighed. She slid down his body like a liquid hug, and he let her wash over him. His shirt was thin, and the warmth of her radiated over him. She didn't move; instead, she pushed her shoulders back into a prim posture. Her breasts pushed forward in answer, and he stepped back, instantly regretting it.

He cleared his throat. "Yes, well, here we are."

"Thanks again," she repeated.

This is when you leave, the irritating voice in his head advised.

"I'm going to go check in on the kitchens. Smelled

some biscuits. Do you need me to come back and help you down the stairs?" He wasn't sure why it was important to him that she did in fact want his help.

Her attention focused instead on her ankle. A nice swell had set in. "I think it's just a sprain, likely not even that, just a little twist. Really, I'll be fine. But maybe we could do the tour tomorrow?"

He exhaled, unaware he had been holding his breath for her answer. "Right, then, yes. For breakfast… I'll get you in twenty?"

"I thought you were meeting your team?" She was biting her lip and it awakened a hunger in him to do the same. *Right. The men.*

"I'll shoot Roger a text, it's fine."

It was amazing, the facility with which he lied. He wasn't at all sure it would be fine. At the moment, he just didn't care. He wanted to carry her down the stairs. Watch her eat breakfast. Watch as she tried to joke with his niece.

Mary smiled at him, shyly. "Twenty minutes, then."

"Twenty minutes." He nodded and left.

Five

Twenty minutes seemed more than enough time at the onset of his mission. Now? Nick stiffened in front of the door to her office.

Amelia Hartmann ran the hospitality division of Hartmann Enterprises. She was clever, Harvard-educated and his younger sister. She was also the current head of the family coalition poised to break up the Hartmann Homestead into smaller parcels to sever and sell, although, for the life of him, he struggled to understand why.

Hartmann Ranch, while palatial in size, proved time and time again too small to house all the strong personalities in their family tree. But it was big enough for him and Amelia. *Just.* Or so he'd thought.

He looked down at the two coffees he held, second-guessing his instinct to mend fences with his younger sister. She was the more difficult of the twins, but Evie was in California and Nick was unprepared to grovel over video chat. The second step—after winning over Alix—in turning the tides on his sister's current plans was mending fences, a chore he'd hated since adolescence but had learned was a necessary evil once he'd unwillingly assumed the leadership of the Hartmann family.

"I'm working on it, just give me time."

A quick glance down the hallway confirmed he was alone, and despite himself, he pressed an ear to the door. He recognized the voice to be Amelia's. She must be on the phone.

"I know…Yes, but there's nothing we can do about it. It's a waiting game. The girl's here now…Yes, with a tutor."

He grimaced. *Amelia.* She always seemed to find out his secrets.

"Give me some time…Don't worry, we're on track with our deal."

Deal? He waited two minutes, then knocked.

"Come in." This invitation was cool. Her persona reverted to the calculated calm she effused into her everyday activities. The sister from his childhood was but a faint memory as he entered the office to face her now.

"Thought you might want one of Pierre's lattes. We just got the new beans in from Ecuador." He offered the cup in her direction, swallowing his pride at the obvious peace offering it represented.

"I'm already caffeinated, thanks." She dismissed him without eye contact, but he lingered.

Amelia sat behind an oversize notary desk, large horn-framed glasses low on her nose. Lush brown hair fell around her shoulders, and in the early-morning light, it occurred to Nick his sister was young for the responsibility she shouldered.

She shuffled a stack of papers. "Can I help you with something else, Nick? I've got a seven thirty with Sebastian to go over our fall bookings. We've got the Saudi prince in again for a month this summer, complete with his entourage, and there are some issues boarding horses."

"They're bringing their horses?" Nick drew a hand to his chin, scratching it. The nice thing about Amelia's take-charge attitude was he hadn't the faintest idea about the minutia of the hospitality arm of their business. He only saw the overview, the numbers, a net positive. The guesthouse, a second palace in its own right, was on the other side of the estate, over an hour's ride away, and that was assuming a steady canter. Amelia split her time between the properties, but whenever an entourage would rent out the entire space she came back to the main house, preferring the privacy. He shifted his weight from foot to foot.

"I'm headed off, then. Alix is settled in." He added it as an afterthought.

"I know. I met her last week. In New York." Hazel eyes flashed at him, and he swallowed back the guilt he felt rising up his neck.

So what if he'd avoided the funeral? He wasn't going to pretend things were okay between him and Austin, much less between him and Katherine. "I'll not apologize for that."

"No one's expecting you to," Amelia fired back, the words hitting him like an insult.

Fine. He'd tried being nice. It didn't matter. With Alix here, he didn't need to make things right with Amelia and Evie. He held the majority vote now and the sale of the ranch was canceled. End of story.

"Nick, the lawyer's on the phone." It was Samantha, his executive assistant.

His office, recently renovated, was the perfect place for him to work. Tucked in the eastern wing of the ranch was a small suite of eighteen offices, where his heads of imports, domestic sales, export strategy, marketing and finance met weekly. The main offices were also on Hartmann land, about thirty minutes' drive from the ranch, and ten minutes from Bozeman, but Nick preferred to work from home as often as responsibilities permitted. With Alix's arrival, he would spend more time here.

"Nick here." He picked up the phone, anxious to hear what the lawyer had planned.

"It's all in order with the visa request," Saul Kellerman promised. In thirty-two years, Nick had never met a lawyer he liked. Saul Kellerman offered no exception to the rule, but he was a necessary evil.

From the corner of his eye, Nick caught Samantha's stare and swallowed. He managed to mumble agreement at the appropriate pauses in his lawyer's diatribe and wrestled himself from the conversation. Samantha shifted, waiting.

"Samantha, I'm glad you stayed."

She took another step toward him, beaming. She was attractive, sure, except for the ever-present element of trying too hard. Maybe it was the heavily lined cat eyes batting a few times too many in his direction in a given minute. They left him with the impression she was trying to remove debris from her eye. Or perhaps it was the red lipstick, a shade too bright for her pale complexion. A flash of red that should have triggered a warning, through the haze of a whiskey-inspired bad decision. It was a mistake he regretted, and one he'd never repeat.

"Of course," she simpered.

He drained his latte, setting the cup back on his desk. He cleared his throat. "I wanted to talk about last week."

Samantha took a few more steps toward him before sinking into a chair. The pleather pencil skirt she sported screeched against the leather of the wingback and he stiffened. She blinked in quick succession as was her habit and parted her lips.

"I am sorry. About the kiss. I know it's not an excuse, but I'd been drinking." He met her gaze and withheld a smile. He didn't want to leave any room for misinterpretation.

Her expression froze, the only movement a twitching nostril. He could see her jaw jut out, then pull back with a hard swallow. She didn't say anything.

This was awkward, but necessary. With Alix's arrival, he hadn't had a chance to speak with Samantha privately since that night.

"You'd been drinking." She repeated his excuse in a flat cadence.

"As I'm sure you noticed." He met her flat tone with his own.

Samatha stood, and made her way to his minibar, pulling at the recessed fridge. She served herself a sparkling Perrier. "Want one?"

Nick picked up his hat and twirled the rim around his index finger before setting the oiled Stetsen back on his desk. He wasn't convinced his message had landed. "Samantha, I want you to know how much I value our relationship—"

"Me, too." She doubled her pace and stood far too close to his desk moments later with a second Perrier.

"Our *business* relationship." He clenched his teeth as he accepted the water bottle.

"I know you have to say that," she said softly, voice pinched. "I'm your secretary, the optics are terrible."

He cleared his throat, swallowing the memory of the kiss they shared a week ago. As drunk as he'd been, he hadn't let it go further, but he couldn't help but wonder—if it had been Mary, would he have pulled back?

He swallowed the thought; the slipup with Samantha was explainable. He'd been struck with grief, drowning sorrows in a bottle of JD. He'd made a mistake, but he wouldn't repeat it. Not even with the tempting tutor. "It's more than optics," he corrected. "The last thing I want is a relationship right now."

She smiled, winking at him. "Who said anything about a relationship?" And she left the office, brushing past the newcomer at the door to meet with him.

Mary Kelly was there, face drained of color. *How much had she overheard?*

"I was just coming to bring you this, er…a proper lesson plan." Her voice was bubbly but thin.

She entered his office and offered a thin stack of white paper embellished with notes and stickers. New information: Mary had a penchant for gel pens.

"Thanks." He accepted the stack and debated for a moment whether he should explain Samantha. "She's… Things are…" He paused.

"You don't need to explain anything to me." Mary shrugged. Her smile was easier than Samantha's. There was, however, something in her expression that left him with the definite impression he did indeed have explaining to do.

Rose willed herself to maintain her smile, mentally chastising herself for walking past the secretary's empty desk to knock on Nick's office door. To be fair, he'd asked her to drop off her notes after breakfast. She'd nodded, temporarily bolstered by the confidence she'd felt since applying her apricot lipstick. Pursing her lips, she'd stalled upon hearing the voices muted by the door. It wasn't closed, and she heard the succinct apology clear as a bell.

"I'm sorry about the kiss."

Her heart beat so quickly at the admission she felt it in her throat. It was Nick's voice.

She shook, wondering about the identity of the woman.

She wasn't left to wonder long, although the time

stretched with punishingly slow seconds. She pressed her thumb against her wrist in an effort to pace the time with her own pulse, but it raced too fast.

Then an overpowering smell of Dior perfume hit her as Samantha walked past. Rose's eyes smarted at the perfume and the cold-shouldered departure of Nick's right-hand woman.

He sat at his desk, cowboy hat casually on the front corner. Funny the things she noticed now, in her distracted half focus, in her determination not to feel anything about that apology. There were a lot of horses in the room. Lithographs of stallions, a bronze cast of a galloping yearling, a copper bookend of a rearing stallion.

Nick was hot, as usual. Dressed in a white V-neck shirt and fitted blazer, she could see the ridged outlines of his muscled body. It was hard not to begrudge a smidgen of sympathy to the poor woman who'd just left. It was impossible not to want him. But Rose? She swallowed her disappointment. Hotshot CEO and his executive assistant? She willed herself not to roll her eyes.

Instead, she pushed aside the tumult of emotions she hadn't expected and got to the point. "I was hoping we could maybe chart out your family? The next unit in Biology is genetics and I was thinking we could make a family tree, dominant versus nondominant traits." Despite her resolve of just seconds ago, she swallowed back the blush heating her cheeks at the word *dominant*. *Was he?* His bottom lip widened into a half smile, betraying a dimple. *Definitely*.

"Sure. I'll dig around for some stuff. Maybe we could sort through it tonight?"

"Tonight." She nodded and reached out to pet the back of the bronze yearling on his desk, a quick rub for luck.

"Excellent." He smiled again. His phone rang but he made no move to answer it.

"You can answer."

"Sometimes saying nothing *is* an answer." He nodded, still making no move to pick up the phone.

Swallowing her retort, she turned and left. His muffled voice still ringing in her ears.

"The last thing I want is a relationship right now."

The admission was not surprising, but she was surprised at her reaction. Just as well she left the room without so much as a "see you later." *Sometimes saying nothing is an answer.*

Six

"You know, I forgot how crap year eleven was," Rose said with no filter, and the teenager next to her snorted in surprise.

"Aren't you a tutor? Are you supposed to say things like that?" Alix Hartmann was trying very hard to give the impression she didn't care one whit about school, but Rose read the underlying urge to please that she herself had suppressed at the same age.

"No, I suppose not." She twirled a pencil around between her pointer finger and thumb as she spoke. "I'm meant to pretend Hemingway is clever and superfun to read. Thing is, I never did like these books. Give me a Mills and Boon romance any day. These old classics are boring sometimes, aren't they?" She smiled conspiratorially. "I was thinking, we could give this a quick look?"

Rose had dithered about whether to admit to the SparksNotes she'd brought along, but after five minutes of trying to dissect *The Old Man and the Sea*, she was ready for the crutch.

The two women sat on the oversize sofas in the second sitting room. The sullen teenager brightened at the suggestion they work from the couch instead of the "guest office" her uncle suggested.

"SparksNotes? Couldn't we just look it up online?" Alix raised an eyebrow, and Rose bit back a snort of her own. She was starting to feel old. The fact that her charge's main objection was the *method* in which she suggested taking the easy way out versus the general rule-breaking stung.

"At least this way we're still reading a book. I was thinking a little cross and compare might be a good idea?"

Alix accepted the well-worn copy of the summary. She cracked the cover and frowned at the inscription on the first page. "Rose Kelly?"

Rose inhaled. She should have scratched out her name. Very unstealthy of her.

"Who's Rose Kelly?" Alix followed up, interest piqued by Rose's stalling.

Clearing her throat, Rose set the glass of water she'd been holding down on the table in front of her. "Rose Kelly is my sister." She grimaced at the lie and added in another qualifier for good measure. "*Was* my sister."

"Was your sister?" The teen studied the inscription.

What a tangled web. Rose's head spun. "Yes. She died. About a month ago."

Alix was quiet. She bent her head forward, as though a nearness to the scratched name would give her a better sense of the woman behind the words.

Not likely.

"She was my big sister. My only family, really." Rose wondered why she added the last bit of explanation. It was both hard and easy to talk about her sister. A confounding twist of opposing feelings, but the overriding taste in her mouth was comfort.

"I lost my parents, too. I guess you know." The girl didn't raise her eyes from the page.

Yes, I know. It's why I came. Rose didn't move. She didn't want to scare away the moment. Instead, she just answered, simple yet honest, "I knew. I know."

Alix flipped the pages of the notes like they were a flip book, checking for further inscriptions among the pages like a child on a treasure hunt.

"I figured," the girl added, putting the book down.

"I'm sorry." Rose didn't add any flowery sympathies. She hated hearing them herself and figured Alix would, too.

Alix pulled a sheet of lined paper from an open binder and started sketching a flower in the absent way a person doodles to pass time. She outlined the twisting vine of a climbing clematis, shading in a leaf. Rose sat beside her, allowing the gift of a few minutes of silence.

"Aren't you going to ask me about it, then? How I feel?" Alix's voice was small, and Rose couldn't tell whether she hoped for or against that outcome.

Rose picked up the hardcover copy of *The Old Man and the Sea*. "Do you know what it's about? This book?"

Alix didn't look up from her clematis, just shook her head.

"It's the struggle between an old man and a fish. He spends eighty-four days trying to catch the fish."

"Does he get it?"

"Did you ever think, sometimes getting what you want is the worst punishment of all?" Rose whispered the thought, as much to herself as her adolescent charge. That was the crux of her problem. She couldn't get Nick, no matter how much she wanted him. Being with Nick meant risking Alix. It meant risking the kids in India, and her chance to make her sister's memory mean something. Getting him would be the worst punishment of all, an exquisite torture worthy of its own SparksNotes.

Alix put her pen down. Her eyebrows knit together as she scratched her head. Then the girl frowned.

"Well, I guess it's good I don't want anything, then." She recommended her sketching.

"Sure. That's one way to look at it." Rose nodded.

Alix frowned, looking at the summary again. "Isn't this cheating?"

"Not cheating." Rose reached for a thick manila folder, filled with hundreds of printouts, guidelines and teacher's tips. "It doesn't say anything in here about not using teacher's aids." Rose waved the thick file folder in Alix's direction, a gesture that provoked a quick wave of protest.

"I'll take your word for it."

"Right, so what I was thinking is we give the first three chapter summaries a quick little review, then we chat about it over a London Fog?"

"London Fog?" Against her better instincts, the girl was curious. *Excellent.*

"This drink is a game changer, trust me." Rose thrust the copy of *The Old Man and the Sea* back into Alix's hand. "I've already read it, clearly, so brush up, then read the SparksNotes while I whip us up a treat." She reached for the cane Nick offered her after breakfast, and hobbled her way to the kitchen, leaving a happy-ish teenager in her wake.

She didn't hear him. As the kettle hummed, she focused on the internet iteration of SparksNotes. The student becomes the teacher indeed. She *felt* his presence before she saw any sign of him. He entered the kitchen quietly and stood behind her.

"SparksNotes?" His voice was low and the deep rumble of a laugh spurred one of her own to match.

Blushing, she slammed the phone to her side and stammered, "No, well, yes, I suppose, I just…"

Nick waved her excuses away as he took another step toward her. "It's fine. That old faithful basically got me through high school, why should it be any different for the teachers? I guess keeping abreast of the cheating aids helps you to spot prepackaged answers from students?"

She swore there was a twinkle in his eye that hadn't been there a moment earlier. "Yes, precisely. I read through them to better spot plagiarism." She blushed, fairly sure she would struggle to spell plagiarism let alone spot it in someone's work.

The shrieking kettle allowed her a moment's reprieve from the embarrassment, and she offered, "London Fog?"

Nick was already at the coffee machine, punching buttons and sliding an old mug with cow-horn handles under the dripping espresso machine. "I prefer coffee, keeps the hair on my chest."

She pivoted on her spot, not wanting her thoughts to be easily readable on her face. If the coffee was responsible for the work of wonder that was this man's chest, she would prepare him coffee until the end of days. Or until the end of term, whatever.

"How's it going?" he asked.

"I'm feeling much better. The cane has been a great help." Focusing all her charm into a smile, she beamed at him.

"Good to hear." Coffee in hand, he leaned into the doorframe and watched her froth milk with a whisk on the stove.

"Looks pretty labor intensive, this... 'London Fog,' was it?" He raised an eyebrow at her efforts to aerate the milk. She turned her attention back to the task at hand, but he was not to be deterred. "Here, let me help with that." He stepped toward her and covered the hand on the whisk with his. She could feel him behind her. Close. If she leaned back a hair, she'd be pressed into his chest. Pressed against his hips... Her mouth watered at the thought and she swallowed. Focus on the latte. *Focus on the girl.* Twenty-seven impoverished kids. Yes, eye surgery was the least sexy thing she could think of. Perfect.

"You've got to whisk in tiny circles," she breathed. He nodded, chin brushing against her hair.

"It's taking quite a long time."

It felt good. Standing trapped between him and the stove. Too good. She wriggled away and huffed, "Didn't your mother ever tell you, all good things are worth working for?"

Mary had said it to her often enough; she just hadn't paid any heed to the advice. Until now.

Nick chuckled. "You might have a point there."

Satisfied the milk was sufficiently frothed, she poured the contents of the now screaming kettle into a waiting teapot, eyeing the clock on the oven to track the steep time. Nick stood still, taking in the methodical process. "You take your tea seriously."

She flushed. "I just thought, taking some time to make a nice drink, show I care. I can't teach the girl anything if she doesn't like me."

"Can I help with that?"

"Maybe. I was thinking, your offer to see the ranch would be nice. We could make a day of it?" The three-minute mark on the oven passed and she poured the tea into the bottom third of the mug, topping the cup with maple syrup, steamed milk and foam. Trouble was, she couldn't manage both mugs and her cane, a conundrum Nick assessed rapidly.

"I'll take these for you." He leaned toward her to relieve her of the cups.

Rose sported a smile of her own when she crossed into the living room. Nick had pulled Alix's laptop onto his knees and was squinting into the computer screen.

"A book about fishing? Maybe school isn't so bad." She overheard his commentary on the book choice and couldn't bite back the widening of her grin.

Nick quizzed Alix on the first few chapters, coaxing out questions, and comparing the old man to different rappers he felt were outdated in their own way. His grip on pop culture was impressive. He rattled off the names of several different artists, eventually luring a reluctant smile from the teen.

"You're making me feel old," Rose said, the statement announcing her arrival. "Even though I'm heaps younger than your uncle," she added.

"Heaps younger?" Nick tried out a mocking accent.

"You don't sound British. I hope you can do better than that." She laughed, sinking onto the couch beside him. Her leg pressed against his. She didn't look over at him, but pressed her eyes shut a moment and let herself feel the strength in the limb next to her. It was as close as she was going to allow herself to get to the cowboy, so she wanted to commit the feeling to memory. If this was all she'd ever get of Nick, it might be enough. It had to be. It felt so good to be needed, but even better to belong.

"Not one bit?" He tried again, mouth pursed before his lips broke into a smile. Rose was pleased to see the mirth spread to Alix. She mirrored the teen's smile, then felt her face freeze as she realized she hadn't issued a genuine smile, hadn't felt so close to anyone, since Mary had passed.

Not a bad day, all things considered.

Seven

The horse was a lot bigger than she'd thought it would be, and not as docile as she'd assumed from the movies. Rose took a cautious step backward, bumping into Alix.

"You ever been on one of these?" she asked her charge.

Alix, wide-eyed, shook her head. The bangs of her brown hair fell into her eyes.

Nick walked toward them, chatting with a wrangler. "Thanks for saddling Betsy," he yelled over his shoulder, and the wrangler dipped his hat and lifted his chin before walking away.

"Don't you have a...*shorter* horse?" Rose sputtered.

"Shorter?" Nick spun and looked at her. "You mean like a pony?"

Rose reached a tentative hand toward the muscled

animal, patting the gleaming coat, hot and hard under her palm.

"Don't worry, Mary, this horse wouldn't hurt a fly," Nick assured her as he checked over the straps and tightened the harness.

"I'm not sure this is a good idea," Alix spoke up. Her eyes were glued to her feet.

Nick grunted. "Yep, it is. Thing is, you've been all over New York State, but never Montana, much less Hartmann Estates. You need to see our land. Feel our roots. Plus, I heard about a botany chapter you and Ms. Kelly are gonna review?" He shifted his gaze from his niece to her tutor.

Alix cleared her throat. "I don't think I can…"

"Us girls can do anything." Rose walked toward Alix, crossing behind Betsy.

"Careful." Nick moved like lightning, pulling her away from the rear legs of the horse and hard against him. Seconds later, the horse kicked up, pillows of dust forming clouds where they had been standing. Betsy, a congenial horse by nature, was still a horse.

"You *never* walk behind a horse, especially one you don't know." He spoke the reprimand into her hair and pulled her close enough for her to feel the movement of his lips against the back of her head.

He smelled like pine. Like woods. Sharp and sweet, wild and pure. For a moment, she pressed her eyes shut, and leaned back into his chest. He didn't smell like a frat boy, or worse, a Paternoster Square banker, drunk on petty day-traded success. Nick didn't seem to need or want any validating, but as she stood with her eyes pressed closed, she couldn't help but wonder how it might have been had he wandered into her bar once upon a Wednesday. He tightened his grip on her, the quick burst of pressure bringing her to the present, before releasing her in an abrupt jolt.

"Thanks." She spun around the moment she was free of his grip. *Why did she wish he'd held her a bit longer? A bit tighter?*

"Nope. I'm not getting on that thing." Alix turned and was making her way back to the barn.

"Alix," Rose called after her, "let's give it a try, shall we?"

Alix spun. "I've never been on a horse. Like, never." Her voice was thin and quiet, and a tentative gaze looked up from under her shaggy bangs.

"Why don't you come give the girls some treats." Nick's voice carried as he lifted the flap of his saddlebag, revealing a half dozen apples.

The bribery worked and within thirty minutes both women were on their respective saddles. The horses followed Nick, sauntering down a well-worn path toward the edge of the woods. The first hour of the ride was mostly silent, the horses falling into single file, and the distance proving an apt deterrent to chatting.

Perhaps Alix's fear had given way to awe at the raw beauty of the landscape. Rose focused intensely on the scenery to avoid reliving the hot pressure of Nick's hands on her, holding her close. Landscape. She was going to appreciate the landscape.

Soon, the silence gave way to a quiet background of forest noise. It was easy to lose time in the forest and her stomach reminded her lunch was approaching with a growl she feared could scare the horse.

Nick pulled up, turning his horse with practiced ease. He jumped off, and put a hand in front of Betsy, halting her with a mere hand sign. Alix's horse followed suit, and the two women sat stiffly in the saddle.

"I'm getting hungry. Shall we make camp here? I brought lunch."

He approached Betsy as he spoke. Rose stared, fascinated by the strong hand running down the neck of the horse, who had turned her head for the caress. The hand stopped on Rose's saddle, and he looked up at her and smiled from under his cowboy hat.

"M'lady?" he mocked, in another faux accent.

She accepted his hand, the warm grip all too familiar, and, somewhat ungracefully, whipped her leg over the saddle. Unpracticed as she was at disembarking, she hurled forward only to find herself for a second time since breakfast clutched against the cowboy's expansive chest. All too familiar indeed. Precisely the kind of familiar that would have her staring for hours at her ceiling again. Heat flooded to her face at the thought.

Nick, braced for the launch, balanced in a counter-step to her momentum and pushed her to an upright posture on her own two feet.

"Mademoiselle Alix." Nick then presented himself with a small bow in front of his niece, keeping his mock accent in play.

Alix made no pretense at grace and held both arms out.

The sun was hot against the backs of their necks, birch trees offering little shade but a beautiful silver shimmer to the leafed canopy. Nick's vest was tossed aside, and his plaid shirt opened a few buttons at the yoke, revealing a white undershirt, still crisp and clean.

Focus. On Alix. And the twenty-seven kids she could save.

With that renewed reminder, lunch was an easy repartee. Having prepped a few points on botany, she interjected a few tidbits and was quickly rewarded with a raised eyebrow and smile from Nick, and unwilling curiosity from Alix. Lunch, a mess of hearty sandwiches French style, was easy.

The day passed as they left the birch forest to explore a new creek bed and then a hidden meadow, and twice more, Nick helped the women dismount and explore different surroundings. Was it just her, or had he held her a second longer each time?

The evening fell fast, the air heavy and damp. The horses were on autopilot. Betsy, while certainly amiable, was not bred for speed. She followed Nick and soon Rose saw the ranch. A wrangler was waiting, and after Nick helped her dismount a final time, the wrangler took the leads from all three horses and walked them away without so much as a nod to the group.

"That was all right." Alix kicked at the ground. Rose could see the quick flash of teeth as the girl swallowed her smile.

"Good. Glad you liked it." Nick's answer was warm, and he leaned against the white fence, gleaming with fresh paint in the pink hue of the setting sun.

Alix walked away, rushing toward the house, kicking at any rock large enough to find purchase against her shoe.

Rose smiled. Today had been a good day.

"Did you want to have a drink after dinner?" His question came out of nowhere.

"With you?" she clarified.

"With me." He pressed against the fence and propelled his weight forward, turning to face her. "I thought we could talk about how you girls are settling in."

"As long as you're not going to grill me about my qualifications?" She smiled. *Best defense is a good offense.*

Nick smiled, too, then whistled and walked toward the house, leaving Rose to scramble behind him, two paces making up each of his long strides. *A good offense might be exactly what she needed.*

He didn't know what had provoked him to issue the invitation. He'd regretted his kiss with Samantha, finding little comfort in his offered excuse of the drunken haze, yet here he was, proposing an invitation to blur the lines of yet another working relationship, this time with not a drop of whiskey to be held responsible. Nick swallowed, but couldn't find even an ounce of regret at having asked her, propriety be damned.

Mary had begged for a few minutes to "wash off the dust," and had taken dinner in her room, but when she resurfaced for the promised drinks, pacing in front of the door to the sitting room, she looked like a new woman. Her hair fell softly on her shoulders, a gold halo of curls, and her eyes sparkled under a modest application of makeup. Barely there, but there nonetheless. *So she cared to look nice.* He couldn't decide if he should embrace the warmth that it made him feel, or push it away.

With his left hand, he held forward her Scotch, amber and sparkling in the firelight.

"Thanks," she answered as her fingers brushed against his in the transfer. The brief touch sent a shock through his system, just as it had every time he'd touched her all day. She was dangerous, because in this moment, he wanted her more than he wanted to save the ranch. Which was a lot.

She circled the room like a cat, elegant but wary, until she sat on the love seat, her cream shirt a sharp contrast to the darkness of her jeans.

She took a sip of her drink. "You work in here?"

He took a deep drag of Scotch before confirming with a succinct, "Yep."

"With your...secretary." She chewed on the last word as though it tasted sour, pulling her lips tight.

"We have an office in town, but a few key people work here at the house with me." The fire lit the room in a warm glow, and he walked over to the love seat, sinking beside her. The down filling of the couch sank under his weight, and their bodies slipped closer together. It was a subtle difference, but it did not pass unnoticed.

"You've been working from home a lot these days," she observed, swishing her drink and watching the Scotch swirl in centrifugal motion.

"Alix has been expelled from three schools. I figure it's best I'm around. As much as I can be, anyway." He looked up at her, meeting her gaze for the first time that evening. "It has occurred to me that I don't know much about you?"

"Who's asking? Nick? Or hotshot CEO of this ranch?" She tilted her head back and let out a short laugh.

"Does it matter?"

"I guess it matters or I wouldn't have asked." She straightened and drained her glass.

"Careful, the lady bites." Nick reached for the bottle of Scotch, tilting it toward her in invitation.

She inclined her glass in his direction. "Careful or you won't find out."

Did he want to find out? One look at her plump lower lip and he swallowed. Yep. Despite the promise of a heap of trouble. Despite knowing it was a bad idea. He wanted to find out.

After filling her glass, he topped off his own. "So if I were to ask, then, what would I discover?"

She took another sip, then looked at him squarely. "I'm a good listener." The pronouncement was laced with suggestion.

"Is that so?"

"It is." She nodded.

"Heard anything interesting lately?" He focused on keeping his face impassive, in an effort to appear disinterested.

She shrugged. "I heard about the kiss."

He choked on his Scotch. "Damn it." He stood, figuring it might be easier to focus without her thigh pressing into his on the damned couch.

Mary looked at him, eyes wide. The knowing tone

was gone, and she once again seemed younger. He wasn't sure why it was important to him to correct her misconception. Maybe because of her role in Alix's life now? Because he didn't want to fall into the same profile his father had shouldered, womanizer and liar? He took another sip of Scotch before deciding the "why" didn't matter much. At least, not right now. He sat back down beside her.

"Yeah. We kissed. Once." To his own ears, his voice sounded hollow. Beside him, Mary leaned back into the pillows of the couch.

"Once," she repeated, rolling the word around in her mouth.

"Ignited by grief. Fueled by alcohol. It never went further and it won't ever go further. I'll admit it was never about her. I don't feel that way about Samantha. It was a mistake."

"A mistake," she repeated again. She leaned away from him. The strip of leg that had been pressed against his only moments earlier was now primly pressed to her other leg. Away from him.

He wished he could read her mind. Or know his own. He cleared his throat. "To be honest, when you're sad—"

"A mistake might be enough." She set her glass down on the side table, artfully landing it in the center of a cork coaster, and clasped her hands in her lap. "I know what you mean." Her legs angled back toward his.

"Together is better than alone." He spoke the words softly, for his own benefit.

"Until it's not." She nodded, then shifted her posture to mirror his, her leg once more an unwitting distraction.

He finished his Scotch and stood again. It felt as though she was looking through him. Another glass of Scotch might lead to more, and he needed to keep all his faculties intact. He wanted her enough to recognize the danger. "I better call it a night." He clenched his jaw and tilted an imaginary hat in her direction.

She stayed seated, smiling at him. "Thanks for the drink, and the company."

"Yep." He turned and left. The walk to his bedroom was endless. Their words echoed through his head. *A mistake might be enough. Together is better than alone.*

In five minutes, she'd sliced through his bravado, and he wasn't sure he liked the naked vulnerability she'd uncovered.

Eight

"You think you're pretty smart, don't ya, Nick?"

The woman on the other end of the phone was angry, her voice abrupt and oddly high-pitched. Nick didn't need the caller ID to identify her. He'd known Katherine's sister as long as he'd known Katherine.

"Franny, nice to hear from you." He eyed the clock and waved away his assistant. Samantha rolled her eyes and gesticulated wildly toward her calendar, but then left, shutting the door behind her.

"Don't you *nice to hear from you* me," Franny threatened, her voice carrying a faint metallic quality as he shifted her to speaker. He struggled to find focus this morning, his head clouded with thoughts of Mary. *A mistake might be enough.* With her, it might be a mistake, but if he could lose himself in her, he was willing to bet it would be transcendent. Question was, would he bet the ranch to find out?

"I'm sorry I haven't called," he started. At least that much was true. He owed Franny his sympathies.

"Obviously, you wouldn't call after what you've done."

"What's this I've done?"

Franny, expounding on her earlier accusations, continued, "If you think you're going to get away with this, you won't. I've got a lawyer."

"Is this about the will?" He jabbed at the phone and took her off speaker, pulling the phone to his ear.

"The will? You mean the unwitnessed document they both *allegedly* signed? Not likely I'm upset about that now, is it?"

"Sounds like an easy enough matter to clear up. Let's not get too upset about it now." Congeniality was not his strong suit, but his mother had instilled in him the ideology that if it was possible to avoid court, you should.

"If you think I'm going to stand by, while my flesh and blood, my own niece, mind you, is used for your advancement—"

"Listen, Franny, just say what you want to say. I don't have time for this."

"What I'm saying? I want custody of *my niece*. You're a bachelor, no better than your father. The courts are more likely to side with a woman than a workaholic control freak of a man."

"Easy there, Franny. I have everything needed to care for Alix, and there's no need for name-calling."

"Everything? Before or after you take care of your precious ranch?"

"I hardly think employment is a barrier to fatherhood."

"*Employment?* Manic obsession with governing your empire more like it."

"Sure, Franny."

"Let's see what the court thinks," she shrieked before disconnecting.

He put the phone back in its cradle and brought both hands to his temples. Pressing a knuckle into the space on his cheek beside his ear, he rubbed in circles to ease the muscle swollen from the clenched jaw he'd sported for the past two weeks. She wanted to petition for custody? Not good. Desperate people made for dangerous opponents.

Between getting to know Alix, wrestling with his desire for Mary and now this…

He needed a break. A boys' night.

Picking up the phone, he dialed the only number he knew by heart, relieved when it was answered on the second ring. "Buddy, can I interest you in a beer?"

"Always," was Ben's quick answer.

"Want to head over? Crack a cold one?" Nick eyed the setting sun, the sky violent pinks and reds. It was late enough to justify drinking, and today felt like a string of Mondays all boiled into one.

His friend didn't answer. "If you're nodding through the phone, I can't hear you…" Nick called out his best friend's habit with a smirk.

"Yeah, why not. I'll come over—can't wait to meet this British tutor. So what's the verdict, then? Is she hot?"

Is she hot? Hot didn't even begin to cover it. "She's out of bounds, buddy, don't even think about it."

"Excellent, so she *is* hot."

His friend disconnected, and for a moment, Nick felt a wave of jealousy. It was unfamiliar. He wasn't the jealous type. *Or was he?* If Ben so much as held Mary's hand a moment too long, he would not be happy about it.

"What's got you peeling labels today?" Ben, his affable self, gestured toward the two empty beer bottles, both naked of their branding. They'd escaped to the gin deck outside, a flagstone patio Nick put in himself after his mother moved out. He'd worried initially about how he'd transform his childhood home into an adult bachelor pad. There were entire wings of the home he never entered, a ballroom for one, that did nothing but collect dust. Step one in his bachelor update? Make an area to drink with the boys. Well, with Ben.

The contractors had finished a few months ago, and a rough granite patio spread to the edge of the infinity pool. An oversize barbecue was far enough from the firepit the chef could prepare dinner, now treating them to the tantalizing aromas of dry ribs, while affording some privacy for their conversations. He grinned. Yes, the patio was a huge *Nick* upgrade.

"Francesca called."

Ben let out a low whistle. "You coulda led with that."

Nick wrinkled his nose in distaste. "I guess burying the lead is more my flavor. Didn't want to sour your impression of our newest houseguest." He nodded toward Mary, who'd turned on like a light when Ben arrived, shining and bright. Or had she lit up upon seeing *him*?

Mary was quick to accept the invitation, agreeing to

join them with a smile. She was nursing her own beer in an outfit of a relaxed plaid shirt tied in a knot above the top of her jeans. After one look at the bombshell, Ben insisted she join them. Mary hesitated only a moment. When Nick smiled back at her, she nodded. *She was a barmaid before. A professional flirt. The glances mean nothing. This woman is your employee, and more importantly, Alix's tutor.* She was the one person in Alix's life to invest consistent time in the kid, and he was not going to undermine that relationship. He couldn't.

"Who's Francesca?" He felt the low vibration of her accented speech in his gut. Or was it somewhere lower than his gut?

Heat pulsed between them, a static awareness that crackled in the air. Her voice, low and warm, cut across the night air like a hot knife through butter. One of the things he loved about Hartmann Homestead was the quiet in the early evenings, and the space it now left for her. No suffering through perpetual traffic and onerous city sounds, here they had a backdrop of babbling brooks and singing birds. Now, the quiet served only to amplify his desire.

"His prom date's sister," Ben answered.

"My late sister-in-law's sister," Nick corrected. He watched her face carefully for a reaction, but her expression was a mask hiding her reaction.

"*Your* prom date married your…brother?" she clarified. Ben started a fire in their firepit, and the flames warmed her features. She looked stunning in her relaxed interpretation of Western casual.

"The way we tell it, his brother impregnated his

high school sweetheart," Ben joked in a vain attempt to lighten the mood. Nick glowered at him.

"That's a lot to unpack," she answered quietly.

"That's how Alix came to be," Nick added. "Also how I ended up the uncle to a sixteen-year-old. Everyone was young then. Too young to make good choices, I guess."

It was nice she knew about the history between him and Alix's parents. True, the gory details were still his alone, but at least she knew the picture-perfect ranch wasn't quite so picture-perfect. Maybe she'd guessed it from his family's absence.

"What did Francesca want, then?" Mary asked.

"Alix." He recognized he was back to his one-word answers. A regression, sure, but given the circumstances, he was doing pretty darn well.

"Can she do that?" Ben cut in.

"No." He answered too fast. "I'm not sure. I don't think so?" His attention was focused on Mary. She blanched at the news.

"What did she say exactly?" Ben pressed.

"I don't know...she was going on about how I wouldn't get away with it." Nick cleared his throat and moved his chair back under the guise of getting away from the smoke. Really, it was to be closer to Mary. He'd always liked playing with fire.

"I doubt it will be that easy," Ben mused.

Nick nodded. "Not much I can do about it tonight, anyway."

"I'm starting to get hungry," Mary quipped.

It was a blatant effort to change the subject, and Nick

was grateful for it. He grinned at her. "Me, too." He was hungry for more than dinner.

The sound of metal dragging on granite caused him to jerk his head up. She was dragging her chair nearer. Closing the last few inches, she parked her seat beside him. She feigned a cough, then smiled. "You look nice tonight."

Ben whistled. Pierre, the resident chef, interrupted the opportunity for further teasing. "How would Monsieur like his ribs?"

"Dry and spicy," Nick answered, breaking eye contact with the tutor as he offered instructions to the chef.

"Madame?"

She blushed with an answer she seemed to choke on. "Wet, please."

Suddenly his own mouth was dry. "You heard the lady." He dismissed the chef. "She likes hers wet."

The barbecue area was several feet away; however, the scent of glorious ribs soon assailed their senses, offering a mouthwatering backdrop to Ben's narration. Bless him for having the presence of mind to supply a stream of small talk. He was a good friend, because at the moment, all Nick could hear was *"wet, please"* on loop. At least Francesca and Alix were now officially the last thing on his mind.

The ribs were excellent. Better than excellent. He was famished, and the ribs, while filling, did little to quell the true source of his hunger. She ate primly, wiping her fingers between each rib, hesitating before licking the bones, then rapidly licking her fingers as she watched Ben do the same.

He felt each lick in his gut, sharp and torturous. "Pass the butter," he asked, voice hoarse. His fingers brushed against hers as she obliged, and his guts twisted again.

"This is sinful," she stated. He loved the way she spoke, the way she held on to a word a moment too long. He reckoned she could make any word sound *sinful*.

"Best ribs—your cook is awesome," Ben agreed, oblivious to the tension. Hopefully, it wasn't solely in his head.

"Yep," was all Nick could muster.

Ben rose to leave, professing an inability to eat one more morsel.

"Are you sure? They haven't brought out dessert," Nick asked feebly, not wanting to deter his buddy's departure.

"Looks like you'll be on your own to enjoy dessert tonight," Ben answered in a hushed tone, and nodded toward Mary, who had risen from the table to pace the perimeter of the pool.

"Benjamin," Nick hissed. "She's an employee."

"Right. I'm talking about what happens off the clock, buddy. You like her."

For lack of a better answer, Nick shoved his friend, hard.

Ben stumbled from the momentum and laughed. "Easy, tiger, I wasn't saying anything you hadn't already thought. I'd wager my front teeth on it."

Nick grinned. "Keep your teeth. I'm not going there. Not with the tutor."

His friend reached for his hat and grabbed his jacket. "In all seriousness, maybe you should. She's a nice girl.

A stunner. And let's face it, she only had eyes for you tonight." Ben let out the few bars of a jovial whistle as he sauntered off.

Nick turned and made his way back to the pool. Just to talk. He stopped a few feet from her back, and watched the glimmer of the underlit pool dance on her blue jeans, highlighting a serious asset.

He couldn't. Not with her.

He should leave with Ben, find a bar. Find another woman. Because Mary? If he lost her, he'd lose Alix. And the ranch. Everything he'd ever wanted.

"Your friend is nice." She spoke with her back still to him. All the better to admire her, he supposed.

"Yep, he's a riot," Nick agreed. He closed the distance between them with a few steps, and stood at her side, hands trailing inches from hers. *He could look, he just couldn't touch.*

"Are you worried? About this aunt?"

He paused for a moment in consideration. "Fran? No. Regardless of her argument, and I'm not sure she even has one, I have a better legal team. Well, I will have." It was the benefit of being a Hartmann, and the assets at his disposal as CEO of Hartmann Homestead were prolific.

"That's terrific." She paced forward a few feet, then paused, cocking her head in inquiry. "Did you want to go for a swim?"

He was surprised by the offer. "That's quite the jump—I'd love to get inside your head." Then bit back the rest of his sentence. Truth was, he'd love to get inside a lot more than her head. There was a duality about her. A guarded vulnerability married with a brash confidence he found enigmatic and alluring.

"I meant the water. It's enchanting." She faced him, eyes wide and inviting.

"I'm enchanted all right. Why not?" He smiled. "It's been ages since I've been in the pool."

She didn't answer, but kept looking at him in the same unnerving way she had during dinner. She reached for the collar of her shirt and began unbuttoning. "I thought maybe we'd end up in the pool, and wore my swimsuit just in case."

"Uh, great," he answered, throat dry as he watched her fingers nimbly unbutton the rest of her shirt, moving to the waistband of her jeans before she shrugged the shirt off.

She wiggled out of her jeans as he watched. "You wearing a suit under all that?" she asked.

He swallowed again in an effort to shake his stunned feeling. It was hardly the first time he'd seen a woman in a bikini. "No, just give me a minute. I keep a suit in the cabin." He nodded toward the cabana a few feet away from the patio. He was stuck between wanting to move as quickly as possible and not wanting to miss even a moment of her undressing.

When he returned, she was already in the pool. Opting against a cannonball, he dived into the deep end, both figuratively and literally, surfacing a few feet from the bathing beauty.

"So, Oxford, how are you liking Montana?" The question was trite, sure, but in the close quarters of the pool, he wasn't ready to voice what was really on his mind.

"It's nice to get away." She dipped her head underwater and turned a clean spin, coming up for air closer to him.

"Anything in particular? To get away from?"

Her eyes were the same color as the water, a clear blue, bright as a night sky.

"Yes. For me there is, anyway." She disappeared back underwater, an elusive mermaid. So she was fleeing something. Someone, maybe. His gut tightened as a flash of white leg swam by, circling him underwater, the best kind of shark. He dipped under and gave chase, grabbing at an ankle.

"Gotcha, mermaid." He laughed as she surfaced. But she wasn't laughing.

"My sister died. Just a month ago. I don't talk about it. Not sure why I'm talking about it now." She was quiet, but her stream of consciousness hit him hard. Her sister. His brother. The unfairness of it all.

He didn't know what to say, so he took a step toward her, then in quick decision, another, closing the gap between them and pulling her against him in a hug. To be fair, it felt like he didn't have a choice. His body decided for him.

She was stiff but melted into him the moment she seemed to realize the hug was given without expectation.

He wasn't sure who pulled away, but when he looked down, her wide eyes stared back at him. "Thanks," she offered.

"I didn't know. About your sister. I'm real sorry."

The pool was underlit, with recessed pot lights offering an otherworldly glow.

"I'm okay. Nothing being sad will fix. I suppose it's normal not to be feeling aces at the moment." She sniffed and lowered her shoulders into the water.

"Sure. I get it." He nodded, and followed suit as she sank farther into the deep end of the pool. "So what made you want to be a tutor?"

She stilled, then spun to face him. "I basically raised my sister. You know, helped her through school, helped with all the details of her life. Rose, uh, she was a good kid." Her voice broke at the mention of her sister's name, and he fought the urge to pull her into another hug. Her voice was low, and detached, as though she were narrating someone else's life story, but it was a story he desperately wanted to hear. His stillness prompted her to continue.

"Well, Rose wasn't really a good kid, I guess. I mean, I always thought so, but boy was she often in trouble. Hanging with a fast crowd—that's how they put it in the movies, isn't it? Drinking a fair bit, not just on weekends." She was talking in a full stream now, and he hung on her every word.

"Bit of a wild child, then?" He took a few strokes back, and kicked himself into a hanging float.

"Right. She *was*." Mary sank below the surface, and popped back up a moment later, curls now slick against her head.

It was a clear end to the conversation. Fair enough.

"Montana sure is different," she added moments later.

"Different how?" he wondered aloud.

"It's just so big. Everything here is huge." She bit

back a smile and gestured to him, surprising him with her boldness. He laughed, enjoying the sudden levity between them.

"Guilty as charged," he said.

"I'm really pleased to be here. Working with Alix." The water was cool, and Nick felt a chill set in, but not even a small part of him was ready to get out of the pool.

"Have you done any other one-on-one?" he asked, truly curious.

"No. Maybe it's why I left. I didn't feel like I had a real purpose." She looked away.

Well, that was deep. He swam back to the shallow end in a few quick strokes, and let his legs touch bottom.

"Must be nice. Feeling like you have a choice," he started, unsure where the sentiment had come from.

"What do you mean?"

"I've just always known…this ranch, this place? I would run it."

She didn't answer straightaway, just deepened her regard, tilting her head forward in marked interest. Finally, she spoke. "Quite the privilege, wouldn't you say?"

"I'm not surprised that's how you'd see it, because, yeah, it is. But isn't it worse to get everything you've always wanted, only to risk losing it?" Somewhere the conversation had pivoted, and here he was, spilling his guts to the beautiful Brit in the impossibly small swimsuit.

The ranch was more than a birthright. It was the thing that made him a Hartmann. His dad had made him promise. Maybe he couldn't voice why that promise was important to him. Why he cared. His brothers shrugged off the responsibility so easily, but Nick was shackled by it. His legacy couldn't be losing the thing that had made him. No. He couldn't fail at this. Not even to be with her, the mermaid incarnate.

She smiled her odd half smile and splashed some water at him again. "I don't think you even know all you want, cowboy." She bit her lip, drawing his attention instantly to the one thing he'd wanted since meeting her at the airport. He followed her in a second lap of the pool, catching up to her in the deep end.

"So your brother married your prom date?" She widened her eyes as she issued her question and changed the subject.

"It was a long time ago." He cleared his throat.

"Yes, you're practically ancient, aren't you?" She swatted another bit of water in his direction, which he managed to sidestep.

"Careful, Oxford." He smiled, unable to help himself. It felt good to smile, even more so when faced with the crushing sadness he'd been shouldering for the past three weeks.

"Can you not call me that?" She paused. "My sister went to Oxford. And I don't want to think about her right now." She turned away, and her cold shoulder rocked him. He took a step toward her, and with a hand on her shoulder, spun her around.

Mary's eyes shone and in them he saw a sadness he mirrored. A sadness that broke down his walls and made him feel as raw as she looked. Since they'd met, she'd been a dichotomy of strength and vulnerability, the latter overpowering him now. For a moment, the opportunity to be strong enough for both of them was inebriating, and he reached for her, allowing his hand to rest on her shoulder, her skin hot despite the tepid water. In a flash, the weight of his legacy, the responsibility of his lineage, faded with the prospect of comforting her. At the thought of being more, even just for one night.

Her bottom lip jutted forward and quivered, and she reached for him, putting a hand flat on his chest. He wondered if she could feel his heart thudding against her palm. She took a step closer, the mini wave of water hitting his waist with the movement. It provoked a response that he was unprepared for. The lapping water serving only to whet his desire.

And so he comforted her with a kiss so thorough it rocked him.

Everything he wanted to say he said with the kiss. *I'm sorry. I want you. I'm hurting. Let's forget this.* Her body, hot against his, was a welcome heat to balance the chill of the pool. It was soft and deliciously curved. The perfect answer to his desperate questions.

His tongue parried with hers and she opened to him with an earnestness that rocked him. A soft mew of submission and he lifted her legs around his, his arousal pressed plainly against her. She wrapped her legs around him, the thin bathing suit a poor barrier, and bit gently at his lip.

"I'm sorry," he started.

"Let's not be sorry, not now." Gone was the sorrow; instead, she looked at him with a burning fire that matched his own.

He groaned, hot in need of her. Maybe, for once, it

was okay. To need someone as much as they needed you? And he needed her now, more than he could ever remember needing anything in his entire life.

And then he remembered.

It wasn't right.

"Mary, I'm sorry. I shouldn't have." He pulled away, voice ragged, hating himself for the effort it took to separate from her.

"You're right." Her nose scrunched up. "I don't know what came over me. I'm terribly sorry. I shouldn't have, you must think me—"

She was out of the pool before he could stop her, but he called after her, anyway.

"Mary." The cry went unanswered, as did his need for her.

Nine

"I mucked it up. Badly." Rose sat on the rock, savoring the wet damp of early-morning dew on stone. "He'll think I was pissed—drunk—liquid courage or something of the sort. Damn…" The curse escaped as a sigh. The phone was cool against her cheek, and for a moment it was easy to imagine her sister listening to her message later, and calling her back with sage advice.

Something like, *Just pluck up, Rose. New day, new opportunity to embarrass yourself, let's not waste it, aye? Try and keep your wits, love. Take the chance to be your best self, and act accordingly, blah blah.* Mary always encouraged her to try again. Embrace the day. Gone were the days of rash decisions and living without consequence, she was here to turn a new leaf. Dream a new dream. Mary's dream.

"Worst tutor ever. Two weeks and I'm next to naked in a pool with my employer—" Just like that, the machine cut her off. One message a day. That was what she was allowed. Five minutes to lose it.

She stood and brushed her jeans. Back to the task at hand: tutoring Alix, finding a way to help the lost teenager find a center, finding a way for Rose to make everything up to her sister. She was finishing this contract. Sponsoring those blind kids… She had to succeed. This job was bigger than her. Bigger than how much she wanted the cowboy. It might not *feel* that way but it had to *be* that way.

Rose fought the temptation to sprint the last few meters to the creek, to try her hand at a profuse apology. *No.* She was here to help the girl. Make a difference. Have meaning. Her libido had gotten her in enough trouble, and while this felt different, she knew it wasn't.

A niggling voice persisted. *Well, couldn't I just do both? Help the girl and myself at the same time?*

Doggedly, she turned away from the creek, set one foot ahead of the next and marched back to the ranch.

"Let's try it another way." Rose chewed the end of her pencil. *How can I explain algebra when I barely understand it myself?* "Or maybe, we just hit pause on math for the moment? Shift to a little, um—" she thumbed through her notebook, landing on a highlighted page before brightening to suggest "—social studies?"

Her charge groaned, which provoked a smile. "Not your favorite? What were you hoping I'd say?"

"Music, maybe? No, definitely free period. We had those at school." Alix looked up from her doodling, eyes wide. *There it was, a brief smile. Yes.*

Rose bit down on the pencil, then withdrew it abruptly from her mouth. "I think you'll have to show me about these 'free periods.' I can't seem to remember any in England. We did have physical education class, though. What say we take a little walk about this fancy estate? Try our hand at some botany? That's science-y, isn't it? And if we double-time our pace for a few minutes, we can count the time as PE, right?"

Alix laughed. A full-out laugh. Rose aimed a pillow at her, but it did little to shut her up. Just as well; it was brilliant seeing the girl doubled over in a belly chuckle.

"Come on, then." Alix jumped to her feet.

"Do you think we should bug your uncle to come? He does know the place." The question escaped before Rose had a chance to second-guess herself, and to her surprise, Alix didn't frown. Another step in the right direction.

"Whatever. If you want to, it's fine."

Excellent. "Maybe you can trade in your flats for some trainers, er, sneakers? It's a bit rocky in some places. I was thinking we could walk to the creek?" Despite herself, Rose was excited. In just two weeks she'd fallen irrevocably in love with the terrain of the ranch and she was sure Alix would, too, given the chance. There was something healing about nature.

"Yeah, lemme go get some *trainers*. Meet you in ten?" Alix dashed off. Rose, unsure if the change in demeanor stemmed from actual excitement about getting outside or the fact her algebra lesson had been deferred, smiled, too. And Rose? She made her way to Nick's office, glad to have a legitimate excuse to see him, not that she needed one.

"Where do you think you're going?" Samantha blocked Nick's door, arms crossed firmly at the waist, an impassable, frowning female.

"I was just going to invite Nick, er, Mr. Hartmann, on a little escapade with Alix." Somehow, the executive assistant had a way of making Rose feel she was naughty.

"Mr. Hartmann is in a meeting. He's an extremely busy man."

"Of course, sure. Yes, that makes perfect sense. Right. Well, perhaps I can just let him know we're headed on a break, then?" Rose had no intention of leaving the premises without Nick's blessing, and this was as good a chance as any to finally chat with the man who had been steadily avoiding her all week. Avoiding her since—she reddened—their swim. Their *kiss*.

"I'm afraid I'm going to have to insist you leave. As I've explained, Mr. Hartmann is occupied—"

"I am employed by Mr. Hartmann, and I'll have his permission before leaving with his niece." Rose eyed the woman, then pushed past her.

"Ms. Kelly," Samantha called, but it was too late. Rose stood in the office, in front of his desk, only a few meters from the cowboy magnate himself.

"Mary, I wasn't expecting you." Nick replaced his phone on the receiver.

"Sorry, I was just… I haven't seen you in a bit." Against her better judgment, a hand pulled at a loose curl. It was a nervous tick of sorts, and she fought against it, forcing her hand back to her waist.

Nick's face, lined from fatigue, tightened. "Yes, I'm sorry about that. I've been quite busy with the ranch. We've been branding the calves all week. They're sixty days old now, so we need to mark them—standard practice, really."

"Sounds terrible," she murmured.

"Part of the business. Smell takes some getting used to, but it's not that bad." He pushed away from his desk and stood, putting his hands behind him, looking devastating. She closed her eyes a moment and flashed back to the musky heat she'd smelled on him the week prior. Delicious. *And inappropriate.*

"I'm thinking Alix needs a break. Thought maybe we'd take a walk around the grounds?"

"A walk? With Alix?" His eyes flickered to his glowing computer screen, and then looked beyond her to the desk in the hallway, where the SWAT leader of a secretary glowered at them both.

"That was the general idea." She assessed his posture and smiled. A winning smile couldn't hurt. It was hard, pretending she didn't want him. That she didn't care. A lie, on top of a lie, on top of a lie. Who could keep track?

"Mind if I join you?" he asked quietly.

"Do I mind?" She repeated the question as though the echo was easier to digest. "No, I don't mind."

He straightened and grabbed his hat from beside the

armchair near the fireplace on his way out of the room. Did he have to wear that hat? Somehow it made him look impossibly hotter.

"Those are your best outdoor shoes?" Despite his goal of being as positive as possible around his niece, he couldn't help keep the skepticism from his voice as he watched Mary and Alix file out of the house down the slate steps to join him at the edge of the yard. The *awesome trainers*, as Mary had lovingly proclaimed them, were crisp white. Nick doubted they'd ever seen the wet side of a field, and as he cast a quick glance up at the sky, he frowned. The clouds were heavy. "Looks like it might rain," he voiced his observation.

"Skies are clear, man, don't try and talk me back into an algebra lesson." Alix's tone, normally flippant, was smug.

"I wouldn't dare." He smiled. It was the right call. Joining them. He was coming to spend more time with Alix. It fit well with his plan to get her to love the land, so she wouldn't sell. He didn't come to spend time with *her*.

Or so he told himself.

The trio made good time crossing the field, and inside thirty minutes, they were at the edge of the creek.

"This is awesome," Alix said. The girl knelt and unpicked her now muddy laces. Moments later, she was barefoot and wading in the water. "It's not even as cold as I was expecting!"

"Quite," Mary answered.

"I don't think I ever did get that swim?" Nick ventured. He was kicking off his boots, and rolling up the bottom of his jeans, intent on joining Alix.

"I'd have thought the last swim was memorable enough?" She took the spot next to him on a large log.

Nick picked up his shoes and put them on the log next to hers. "Yeah, I was meaning to talk about that with you."

"I'm so sorry," they said in unison.

He sucked in his breath. "What could you possibly be sorry about?"

She was pulling at the bark of the log, small fingers digging into the deep crevices of the waterlogged trunk. "I just was…" Her voice was small and he placed a hand over her scratching fingers.

"I was the one who couldn't restrain himself. I'm sorry." He tightened his grip on her fingers, and she met his gaze, large eyes beguiling as they widened in understanding. Suddenly he wasn't sure why he had been avoiding her. It wasn't that bad, this truth between them.

"Guys, you're being weird." Alix's pronouncement was accompanied by a splash as the teen chucked a stone in their direction.

He picked up the round rock at his foot and lobbed it back. "You don't know the half of it, kid."

They waded in the creek until their feet were pruned. Then a crack of thunder interrupted.

"How can there be thunder without any rain?" Alix was curious.

This was a great opportunity for a lesson on high-pressure weather systems, and Nick waited for Mary to jump on the chance to turn this excursion into a lesson.

He'd seen the notes on weather in her lesson planning. To his surprise, Mary turned toward him and added, "Yes, why, Nick?"

"Guys, if we don't leg it back, we're gonna be soaked. That's a promise."

Alix shrieked and made a beeline for the creek's edge, her pants now wet to the knee, an ombre effect of light blue jean to dark damp indigo. "Come on, I don't want to get struck by lightning."

Mary, back on the creek-side log, was pulling on socks and sliding into her shoes. "Careful," she called after her charge, "I rolled my ankle about two hundred meters from here."

"Meters? Welcome to *America*, Mary," Alix shot back.

"Play nice, girls," Nick reminded, offering a hand to Mary. "Let's head back—no rush, really, a little rain never hurt anyone."

As they crossed the large field behind the ranch house, the rain fell. It was a warm rain, and after the initial shock of the wet shower, Mary spread her arms as wide as she could and spun with her head rolled back, face staring into the weeping sky.

Alix watched, stunned to silence. "What are you doing?" she asked, adding a private, "She's nuts," as a sidebar to Nick. *Awesome to be on the receiving end of an inside joke.*

"I can hear you," Mary called, still twirling with abandon. "Don't hate it till you try it."

Alix watched Mary, and Nick watched Alix until the young girl shocked him. She spread her arms wide and looked up into the sky, then started spinning as fast as she could.

"Try saying weeeeeeee," encouraged Mary as she turned faster and faster.

"Weeeeeeeeee," called out the girl.

Then Nick did something that surprised even himself. He spread his arms, tilted his head back and spun, howling weeeeeeeee into the sky.

Ten

Nick had started his day with a thick stack of papers and he was ready to call it quits, having made little progress on the pile. Budgets, forecasts, new employee contracts and marketing plans all melded together in an ominous to-do list. Heavy was the head that wore the Stetson today. He needed perspective.

Nick spun in his chair and took in the great expanse of field out the window. The land was beautiful. Wild. Contrary.

Like her.

He picked up the employee contract Saul had emailed over.

The paperwork was in order. Mary Kelly, of London, had signed with a loopy John Hancock in all the right places. Lettered in a neat script was her address and birthday. A Gemini, sure, but he never would have pegged her for thirty-four. Before he could stop himself, he typed her address into Google street view and was zooming in on a townhome in lieu of attending to paperwork.

The door to his office swung open and Samantha entered, swishing her hips and smacking her red lips with invitation. "I got the tickets you asked for." She held out an envelope. "I know we'd just discussed it in passing, but with everything that's happened, I thought you might be too preoccupied to remember how much I like a good rodeo." Her tone was hopeful and eyes shining. *Damn it.*

"I was going to take Alix. Jackson is riding this weekend. I figured we'd take the jet."

And he'd meant to invite Mary.

He'd been wanting to get Mary on the jet ever since her snarky remark in his office about private jets.

"We'd take the jet? Sure, I've got all three tickets." Samantha smiled again and took another step toward him.

In an abrupt swipe of his hand, Nick slapped his laptop shut. No sense making this more painful than it had to be. He'd told Samantha the kiss was a mistake and there would be nothing more between them. Looked like she hadn't believed him. "I'm taking Mary, figured we could add a little statistics homeschooling to the trip."

Her face fell. "Homeschooling, yes, I see. A rodeo seems—" she paused and bit her lip "—very educational."

"Can you get a suite at the Hilton? We'll stay the night, catch up with Jacks."

Samantha nodded.

The night away for Alix had been Ben's idea. "Might as well show her the good bits, if you want her to like it here," he had said. Nick was sure he'd been referring to Alix.

Mary had jumped at the idea of a "real rodeo," and her sheer excitement was contagious.

"Samantha?" he pressed, feeling the need to be crystal clear with her before leaving on this trip.

"Yes, Nick." She smiled at him.

He scratched his chin, then tore off the Band-Aid. "I just wanted to apologize again. About the whole situation. I will never cross that line with you, or with any employee." He said the words, only half meaning them.

She stiffened at the statement, flush fading from her face and her eyes narrowing. "Right. Of course, I understand. No employees, that sounds fair."

He nodded. "Thanks for your understanding, Samantha. I really appreciate it." Nick didn't address the sinking feeling roiling in his stomach at the way she spat the words "no employees." It felt like a threat. Or worse, a dashed dream.

Tonight they were headed out for a surprise. Somewhere "Western," he'd promised last night during dinner.

Rose waited outside Alix's room, but when her knock went unanswered, she pushed the door open. Alix was lying on her bed, staring at the ceiling. Her face was drawn and pale. The kid had been crying. Again.

She stood in the doorway, waiting. She was channeling Nick, and his response to Alix. There was something about his calm patience that she—and Alix—appreciated. It was new to her, just sitting with someone else's big feelings, and in an effort to replicate it, she leaned into the frame. If Nick could convey quiet support that made the listener feel better, she could try, too.

"We're not leaving yet," Alix murmured.

"No," Rose agreed.

"So? What do you want, then?"

"You're not making things easy," Rose noted in response.

"Whatever gave you the idea life was meant to be easy?" Alix shot back.

"Aren't you a bit young for such pessimism?"

"Says you," Alix snarked.

"You know, my parents died when I was sixteen?" Rose bit her lip. She hadn't intended to admit that. Certainly not while sober.

Alix sat up on her bed, pupils wide and staring from under her bangs.

"It's why I took this job. I was gonna say no. But I got the brief, read about you." Rose took a step into the bedroom and put a hand on her hip.

"Isn't this a great job for a tutor?" Alix asked. "I'm guessing it pays better than a lot of others." Alix rolled her eyes and fell back against the pillow.

Rose made her way toward the bed. "I'm not for sale, Alix. I came here because I wanted the job. I wanted to work with you. I'm not even keeping most of the money." She reddened. The admission was another slip.

"What do you mean, you're not keeping the money?"

Alix pulled herself into a seated position on the bed, and eyed Rose curiously from slanted eyes.

"It's not very—" Rose bit her lip, searching for the word "—couth. To talk about money. Let's talk about this rodeo." She was desperate to change the subject.

"What are you gonna do with it?" Alix persisted.

Rose pulled up her phone. She'd been down this rabbit hole with Alix before. When the girl got curious, she was like a dog with a bone. Rose found the pic. The one that had kept her sister up at night. Handing her phone over, she studied her charge.

"Why are you showing me this?" Alix demanded, shoving the phone away. "You could've given me a disclaimer or something."

"Sorry. I know it's graphic."

"What happened to her eyes?" Alix's voice was soft.

"Cataracts. Treated by the local doctor, although the 'doctor' label might be putting it generously." She allowed herself another look. It was a difficult photo. Botching an eye surgery on someone so young was heartbreaking.

"I didn't know you were really into…eyes?"

Rose laughed. "No. My sister had cataracts. When she was a kid. She had the operation, was totally fine." She paused. "My sister who died."

"So you carry the picture on your phone of someone else's botched eye surgery?"

Rose swallowed. The lump in her throat was hard. "Yes. I mean, my sister had childhood cataracts. They were removed and she was fine. But because of the experience, my mom was really involved in a charity that helped kids like these, before she died. And my sister really wanted to help, too. Before she died. So when I got this contract—"

"Saw the paycheck, you mean?" Alix grinned.

"That's a whole lot of eye surgeries, if you know where to go." Rose chucked a pillow at Alix, then cleared her throat.

"So let's do this, okay? Try and have a nice night?"

"A Western night?" Alix cracked a smile. It was as close to a peace offering as Rose could hope for.

"We're bringing a cowboy, aren't we?" Rose smiled back.

"If you'd call my uncle a cowboy..." Alix rolled her eyes.

Oh, yes, she'd definitely call Nick a cowboy. In the best way.

"Just get your stuff. He's waiting."

Alix swung her feet off the bed, and followed Rose out of the home, clutching her knapsack against her as she walked toward the jet. Twenty-seven surgeries. Twenty-seven lives she could change forever. It was a heck of a tribute to her sister, and she wasn't going to mess it up. Not even for a cowboy like Nick.

It wasn't fancy. It was a rodeo. Loud and dirty, with people spilling everywhere. To her surprise, there were as many women as men. Fitted shirts and tight jeans tapered into cowboy boots of assorted colors. Rose felt out of place in her stilettos, wishing she'd pulled on the trainers she'd worn on the jet.

She stood out, and she didn't like it.

Oddly, Nick looked comfortable. He held a Molson and drank from the can.

Giant floodlights lit the outdoor pens, and Nick disappeared in a throng of cowboys, leaving her and Alix sitting on the first row of a metal bleacher.

"I won't be long," he promised.

Alix's eyes were as wide as her own, and she sipped at a Coke, elbows on her knees as she took in her surroundings.

Nick was talking to the cowboy beside the bullpen, clapping him on the back, then turning toward them as the cowboy climbed into the staging pen.

The bronco rushed from the shoot with a ferocity Rose had not expected. Nick, now seated next to her, pushed forward on the bench, knuckles white.

"Something eating you, cowboy?" Before she could stop herself, she put a hand over his.

He stiffened at her touch, then relaxed. "It's my brother." He nodded toward the cowboy in the run.

The run opened and, twelve seconds later, Jackson Hartmann won the buckle.

It was a bad idea, maybe, but he asked her, anyway.

"Do you want to come and see a rodeo after-party?"

Mary nodded. "Give me ten minutes."

Alix, safely deposited on one of the hotel's queen-size beds, was bingeing a streaming teen series. "I'm not moving from this bed again," Alix announced.

So it would just be him and Mary.

Jackson had texted the location, walking distance from the hotel. The bar was packed, with a live five-piece band strumming and beating rhythms Nick recognized. It was too loud to talk much, which he supposed suited his brother just fine. Nick reached for Mary's hand, to pull her through the crowd. Jackson was in the VIP lounge, and the Hartmann name was all it took to join him.

"Nick, good to see ya." Jackson pushed a beer in his direction, which he accepted. The bottle cold and the drink crisp as Nick sampled the local brewery's ale.

"Who's this?" Jackson turned his attention toward Mary, extending a hand. "I'm Brad."

"Brad?" Mary shot a quick glance toward Nick, confusion plain on her face.

"I ride as Brad." His brother shrugged.

"I'm Mary." She smiled, then added, "I tutor, as Mary." Her face spread in a wide grin.

He felt that smile, and judging from his brother's grin, so did Jackson.

They fell into an easy banter, Mary poking fun at *Brad*, Nick nodding along. Buckle bunnies threw themselves at Jacks, who remained aloof despite the ever-present stream of attention. It was odd. Nick hadn't known Jackson to be one to say no to the ladies, but he was aloof nonetheless. Surprisingly, it didn't bother him to see Jacks flirting with Mary. He trusted her.

"You gonna talk about the ranch?" Jacks asked when the waitress arrived with a bottle of Scotch. Following the second glass, Nick felt ready.

"Not much to say. Amelia's working up a storm. I've got some ideas in the fire. With Alix, we've got the votes, so things are all right at the moment."

Jackson took another sip of Scotch. "Don't underestimate Amelia, she's just like Dad." His voice dropped, leaving no mystery as to the intention of his comment. It was an insult.

Beside him, he felt Mary push to her feet. "I need the loo."

He stood, offering an arm, which she shook off. "I am a grown woman. I'll take myself, thanks." With that, she turned and made her way.

"Grown woman indeed. They didn't make them like that when we were in school." Jackson grinned, face relaxing with the joke.

"I'd say," Nick agreed.

Jackson nodded, then tipped his hat off, spinning it around in idle hands.

"So she's tutoring Austin's kid?"

"Alix, you can call her Alix, man. She's your niece, too."

"I know. I've been sending birthday cards." Jackson shrugged. "I just meant, isn't Alix a big part of your plan, with the vote and the ranch…" Jackson reached for his Scotch, eyeing Nick as he tilted the glass back for a deep drag.

"Thanks, Captain Obvious. I mean, sure, Alix is a big part of the plan, you know that." Nick frowned with a deep dislike of where the pointed interrogation was headed.

Jackson's lips drew into a thin line and he frowned. "Right. So be careful. The tutor is gonna have huge influence on the kid. Don't mess this up."

Mercifully, Jackson changed the subject before Nick

could answer, and continued to enlighten Nick with his insights into Amelia. They were colored by a deep dislike of Amelia's husband, Scott.

"I better go see where the tutor's got to," he interrupted his brother after twenty minutes had passed.

A blonde slipped against Jackson and looked up at him with insipid eyes. "You do you, buddy," his brother said with a smile, before turning his attention to the blonde.

The band had stopped playing, and his feet crunched against peanut shells discarded by the patrons as Nick made his way to the ladies' room. He heard her before he saw her, the British accent unmistakable through the din of American chatter.

"No, I don't want to dance," she insisted to a large brute of a man dressed in denim.

"I don't care if you've got a mandate for hospitality, I'm here with someone," she insisted again, louder this time. The man—Nick could only see the back of him—was drunk, but his intoxication offered no excuse for his behavior.

I'm here with someone. Damn right she was.

He didn't think. First, a hand on the shoulder, the grip provoking a turn from the assailant.

"What do you think you're—" The man spun and cocked his fist, but Nick was faster. Blinded with anger and surprised by the force of his feelings, his fist connected with the man's jaw. One punch and the man was on the floor.

Mary hurled herself at Nick, forehead hitting the fleshy muscle under his collarbone.

"Hush now, it's fine," he whispered into her hair. He felt her shake. "Let's get a breath, all right?"

He led them from the bar. Outside, the moon was bright and cast a blue glow on them both.

"Your brother's lovely."

It was clear from her tone that she didn't want to talk about the man who'd grabbed her. That punch still stung his knuckles, but he was willing to let it go if she was. "Sure. Feels like I barely know *Brad* anymore." Despite himself, he rolled his eyes.

"He's just sad." She nodded, and in the blue light of the night, she looked sad, too.

"Shall we?" He gestured toward the hotel, visible from the bar, but about a ten-minute walk away.

"Why don't you tell me about the last time he wasn't sad? Or…maybe about your favorite childhood memory?" She was a little unsteady on her feet, whether due to the Scotch or the aftereffects from that encounter he didn't know. He offered an arm, which she took.

"My favorite childhood memory?" He scratched his chin and set the pace. Normally, he didn't indulge in those kinds of conversations, especially with a woman, but he, too, was feeling the warm buzz of Scotch. "My favorite childhood memory is my back not hurting." He didn't know what else to say.

She was quiet.

"What about you?" he asked.

"My favorite childhood memory is not hurting, either."

He stilled. Putting his second hand over hers, he squeezed. They walked in silence for a few minutes, and Nick allowed his thumb to brush over the back of her hand.

Then her voice was clear through the night air. "Why didn't you do distance learning for Alix? Why hire a tutor?"

So she wanted to change the subject again. "You regretting your contract?"

Her shoulder pulled away from him fractionally. "No, I'm not regretting *that*."

Perhaps it was the way she paused on the qualifier. Perhaps it was the way her eyes widened a fraction as she sucked in a breath to answer. But he knew in that moment he didn't want any regrets, either.

"I'm glad you're here. Real glad." He squared his shoulders and faced her.

"Do you think it's helping? With Alix, I mean." Her eyes were wide, and for a moment, he read the hope naked on her face.

"I didn't know her before. I'm not proud of that, but it's true. But I can tell you, the kid is doing better. And it's gotta be due to you."

She smiled then, wide and optimistic. "Did you ever think, cowboy, this change in her is kinda due to you, too?"

He liked the idea, even if she was saying it just to please him. Then a drop of rain fell, followed by another until the flash storms so frequent in spring left them both wet to the skin and running for the hotel, sheltering in the three-foot overhang of the soffit.

Two minutes later he was bidding her good night in front of her room.

"Good night, cowboy." She smiled. Her eyes sparkled and he stepped closer to her, to make space for a passing room-service trolley.

Her chest heaved with a heavy breath, and in the close quarters, her breasts pressed against him. He'd never been so glad of the service staff in this, or any, hotel. Curiously, she didn't move away. Didn't turn toward the door, just looked back at him, punctuating her heavy breaths with a deliberate bite on her lower lip. She tilted her chin toward him, closing the space between them and parting her lips.

He paused, they'd said this wasn't on the table. No kissing, but how could he not? She breathed, then he pressed a kiss, hot and firm, on her mouth. She tasted of Scotch and strawberries, tentative at first, then ardently returning his fervor. But before she could brush him off, he straightened and nodded. "Good night, then." He had to leave if there was any chance of salvaging the propriety they'd both promised to adhere to. He'd been weak enough as it stood.

She hesitated for only a moment and closed the door.

He stood, staring at her door a moment too long, wishing he had said how he felt. Problem was, he wasn't entirely sure he knew.

The knock came twenty minutes later, so quiet he'd thought for a moment he was imagining it. "It's open," he answered. He was lying on his bed, staring out the window as the cars flashed by, miniature from his penthouse view.

He heard her enter. Smelled her hair, still wet from

the rain. Knew her lips to be hot from the kiss he had pressed on her in a moment of weakness. "You were supposed to go to bed."

"I'm sad." Her voice was evidence of that, wavering and thick with emotion.

He swung his feet off the bed and stood. She closed the distance between them, and there she was, in his space again.

It was a marvel, the way someone could break down your barriers, just by getting under your skin. Getting into *his* skin.

His windows were naked of drapery and the moon lit the room with blue shadows. She was beautiful.

"I'm sad, too," he admitted. It was easier being honest in the dark.

"You kissed me." She stated it as fact, and it was. But what she wasn't saying was more important.

"I kissed you because I wanted to, not because I'm sad. I'd apologize, but I'm not sorry."

She sat on his bed and started unbuttoning her cardigan. He watched, arousal building with each pearl button she released. The last button freed and the thin wool garment fell to the floor. Underneath she wore a thin-strapped camisole, and with a shrug, the straps fell off her shoulders and the camisole pooled around her waist. She shimmied it down over her tights and stepped out of it. She stood, in skirt and bra, and faced him, hooking her thumbs into her waistband. Her eyes, pools of dark blue desire, made contact with his and she deepened her gaze as she unzipped her skirt.

He sucked in a breath. "Are these for my benefit?" He

reached for the matching lingerie, a cherry-red, simple cotton bra and thong. *Very Mary*, he thought. *Simple, and dead sexy.*

"So what if they are?"

"The woman makes a fine point."

"I'm more interested in what kind of point you can make. Naked." Her hands were at his neck, pulling apart the snaps of his shirt, and permitting themselves free-range access over his torso.

"What do you think, Nick? Can you make me feel better?" Her head was pressed into the nook in the top of his chest, and she spoke into his neck.

As though the question awakened him, his hands came alive with a purpose of their own and gripped her against him. He looked at her, and pressed his mouth against hers. It didn't matter that she worked for him. Didn't matter that she was the closest thing he had to a lifeline with Alix, and moreover, his plan to keep the ranch. He wanted to kiss her again. He wanted to make his point, naked.

"I'm ready to try," he promised, refusing to hear the small voice inside reminding him this was a bad idea. She was his employee. Critical for his plan.

And right now, he didn't care.

She sucked in a breath as he kissed the spot on her neck just under her jaw. She was fresh and kind, clever and hurting. An intoxicating combination—he prayed he could handle the hangover.

He didn't know why she was sad. It could be a million reasons. Maybe a better man would have waited. Asked. But he was tired of trying to be a better man.

Her hands, insistent, pulled off his shirt, tracing the lines of hard muscle earned roping and riding. He had never been vain, but in this moment, he was glad of his physique and the confidence it earned him. He caught her wrist before it dipped into his jeans.

"It's a bad idea." His words hung in the air between them. There. He'd said it.

She laughed, a throaty chuckle he felt in his gut. "Is that meant to be some sort of disclaimer?"

She pressed herself against him, her breasts against his chest. The heat a siren call to his libido. "Disclaimer?" he managed to ask. His mind was not working. All he could think of was where she was going to press next.

She didn't answer, just raised a hand to his neck, pulling his head toward hers. Miraculously he paused. Pressing his forehead to hers, he left enough space between their mouths to breathe a thought. "The kiss. Before. It was a bad idea. But kissing you now?" He swallowed, unsure he could stop himself even if he wanted to.

"Are you going to, then?"

"Not kissing you would take more strength than I have." He delivered on his confession. Her mouth yielded, her lips parting at his slightest insistence. She let out a soft whimper.

She pulled him toward her. "I want this. I need this."

He knew then that tonight was outside his own experience. Her admission provoked one of his own. He needed this, too, but true as it was, he couldn't say it aloud. So he answered the only way he could. Tracing a finger over her jawline, he paused at the clenched muscle, pressing a kiss there before assuring her. "You're beautiful."

Her jaw relaxed and he was rewarded with a smile. Just like that, he came undone. His hands gripped her hips, fingers digging into the soft expanse of her thigh. He flexed his hands against her, into her, and she leaned into him.

If there was a woman alive sexier than Mary Kelly, he didn't want to meet her. She was a symphony of curves; but more than that, she was pliable and lithe beneath him, rising to his touch and the chorus of desire it provoked.

He dropped to his knees before her. "Tights off," he ordered. Too impatient, he pulled them down past her knees, following the curve of her calf with a hot hand.

"Yes, sir," she breathed, her voice gasoline to the fire. Her inflection, the daring lilt of the *sir*, powered him forward.

"I think I want your shoes on," he decided aloud. Wordlessly, she stepped back into her heels, legs now freed of the tights. He clicked his tongue in reproach and she kicked her feet apart, forming a triangle with a heavenly apex.

"Yes, sir," she repeated.

He caught her leg and pressed a kiss into the curve of her knee. Then followed with another a few inches higher. "You are mesmerizing," he breathed into her thigh. He ached with his need of her. "I can't remember ever being this hard." Her hands busy in his hair, he felt the tug urging him to his feet. With palatable reluctance, he stood, head filled with the alluring scent of her.

"Hard, are you?" she murmured, free hand now headed in search of plainer evidence.

"See for yourself."

She did, making quick work of his belt, then relieving him of his jeans.

Nick stood naked, watching her take in the sight of him. Her gaze lingered, but she didn't blush. Her eyes, low-lidded, flicked up at him. "So, cowboy, you were saying you might make me feel better?"

Her tone was playful, but Nick read her statement for what it was. False bravado. "Yeah, I reckon I can."

He traced a finger up her thigh and across her slick center. Her readiness as plain as his, he slid a finger into her. She was smooth and wet, velvet heat coating his finger and calling for another. Fingers coated, he raised them in search of a button he intended to make his. She arched into him, nipples hard against his chest.

"I want you so bad I'm gonna burst," he admitted between kisses. His thumb, pressing with what he hoped was delicious pressure, now matched the rhythm of her grinding hips. Her hand reached for him but he pushed it away. In two backward steps he pinned her against the wall of the hotel room.

"If you want me, then take me," she ordered.

"Not so fast," he cautioned, dipping a hungry mouth to her chest. "You're not exactly in a position to boss me around."

"So you like to be the boss, then, do you?" To his surprise, she nipped at his bottom lip.

"I am the boss, and yes, I do like it." He bit her back.

She twisted but he covered her body with his own. Then, in a move that surprised him again, she hooked her legs around his waist.

"Easy, girl." He brought an arm under her and readjusted. Keeping her high on his chest he carried her to the bed. Depositing her, he sprung off the bed, reaching for his jeans.

"You're not getting dressed," she threatened, propping herself up on her elbows.

"No." He grinned, retrieving a condom from his back pocket.

She opened the condom and had it on him quickly. Then she swung a leg over him, poised and paused. Face-to-face, she looked at him, her eyes an astonishing blue. In the dark of the hotel room, they were near-black, but he read the desire. Then with an excruciating slowness, she lowered herself until they were one.

He didn't breathe. Couldn't breathe. Her tightness enveloped him, but it wasn't that exquisite sensation that paralyzed him.

There was a vulnerability about her he could see. He could feel. One he mirrored.

In the blue-gray light of the room, he traced the curve of her chest, fingers light yet insistent. She curled at his touch, but didn't stop her agonizing tempo.

The kisses followed. Hot now, unyielding. Her palms against him, pressing him away and drawing him closer in a contradiction of pressure. He swallowed, determined not to let go. He wanted her writhing on him, and with newfound determination, he gripped her hips and flipped them, covering her body with his own.

"Nick," she said quietly, biting her lip. They had a teenager on the other side of the shared wall.

He kissed her then, covering the next moan with his mouth, his efforts redoubled. He was relentless now. Driving in and out of her as she bucked against him.

"Nick," she breathed again the moment her mouth was free. "Oh God, please soon."

Her spasms were the final nail to his pleasure, hammering a thousand electric shocks through his body. The release was all-encompassing and he shuddered. Dimly, he heard a sharp cry. Felt her pulse around him. Felt a scratch of nails down his back. He savored the pain as it pulled him back to her. He rolled, then pulled her into the shallow of his shoulder.

And for the first time in a long time, he wasn't sad.

She wasn't sure what woke her. Nick was asleep, his slumber well earned. She shifted and stared at him, his face relaxed. The dark shadow of his beard was growing in. Her skin was marked with a red rash from persistent scratchy kisses. Well worth it. His nose was straight, and a long forelock of hair fell in front of his closed eyes. He was unguarded in sleep, but just as difficult to read. He hadn't said any of the things she'd wanted to hear. But she didn't care. Empty words were the last thing she needed; she'd heard them, and said them, enough times before. No, she'd take the actions any day, and what actions they had been.

She wasn't a virgin. Far from it. But she hadn't ever had sex like that before. Her body tingled at the mere memory. He'd woken her twice during the night, and worshipped her. *Worshipped* felt like an appropriate word; his ministrations had brought her close to God. It was scary now. Having another thing she didn't want to lose. No, she self-corrected. She didn't have him. *You can't lose what you don't have.*

If she was careful, they could do this. She could help Alix and be with Nick. She could fulfill her sister's dreams and live this one for herself, too, no matter the doubts she'd had before. Everyone had secrets, and it wasn't like things were going to get serious between them.

This revelation was a good one.

He opened his eyes, the warm brown awakening her cravings. "You look good enough to eat."

His hand, moving under the blanket, trailed up her leg.

"I'd think you'd need a fast after all the feasting last night?"

"I'm a glutton for punishment." He grinned, dipping his head beneath the sheets.

Her hands twisted in the fabric. She pressed her head back into the pillow, squeezing her eyes shut. She wasn't going to think about anything but his tongue. Not that she could have had she wanted to.

"Where do you think you're going?"

She stilled. She'd thought he'd fallen back asleep. Surely the man needed rest? She slipped on her shoes and twisted to face him. "I've gotta get back to my own bed."

"Speaking as your boss, I think you might have other duties to attend to," he joked, rubbing the still-warm spot on the sheets she'd occupied a few minutes earlier.

"Speaking as your niece's roommate, I better get back. I don't want to sneak in after she's awake. Plus, I think you're out of condoms." Her revelation was quiet, but daring.

A shadow passed over his face. "You're right. You should go."

Her heart sank. She wasn't sure what she'd been expecting him to say, but *you should go* stung. He looked at his watch.

"Shit, it's already seven." He was out of bed like a flash.

Standing naked in the daylight, the sight of him weakened her. "Looking good, Mr. Hartmann." She whistled.

"Watch your mouth, miss." His eyes promised a playful threat, and he pulled on a pair of briefs that only heightened his allure.

"I better go," she said.

"See you at breakfast?" He spoke as he pulled on gym clothes. "I'm just gonna find the gym, then I could meet you ladies in an hour and a half?"

Rose nodded, and let herself out of his room. The bed separated them, so there was no kiss goodbye. She didn't want to seem needy. It was fine. She'd had a thousand kisses.

Alix was still asleep when she entered the neighboring room. She sank onto her bed, and opened the drawer of her night table, pulling out Mary's clunky phone. *I've done something.* She didn't speak her admission aloud. Didn't need to. Voicing it didn't make it more or less true.

A quiet knock interrupted her confessional. She opened the door to find Nick.

"You forgot something." His voice was warm and husky.

"Did I?"

He took a step closer, raising a hand to her face. He lifted her chin and met her mouth with his. The kiss was short, sweet and deliberate.

"That's better," he breathed as he pulled away from her.

She hadn't wanted to seem needy, and yet here she was. Needing.

A sound from inside the room—Alix stirring?—made her heart race. And suddenly the *something* she'd done felt like a mistake. The kind of mistake her sister would never have approved of.

Nick studied her, gym bag on his arm. "What's up, buttercup?" he asked.

"This." She gestured at the space between them. "I think we need to remember why I'm here. For Alix." *For Mary.*

He stepped back. Something like hurt flashed in his eyes before it was quickly replaced by nonchalance. "I get it. Let's cool things off. Sure."

She nodded, lips pulling into a thin line. Nick spun and walked away, leaving Rose with the distinct feeling the cooling off was much easier said than done. With the taste of him fresh on her lips, she swallowed, acknowledging after the night they'd shared, a second course might be even more tempting than the first.

Eleven

Samantha stood to the left of him, tapping her foot in a sharp aggressive beat against the floor. *Tap*, *tap*, *tap*.

"What?" He looked over to her, his tone a victim to the annoyance flushing through him that hadn't abated in the two days since they'd returned to the ranch.

"What yourself," she snapped back.

Being around Samantha served only to remind him of all the things he liked about Mary. Surely the decision to *cool off* was premature, but at the same time, her reaction begged the question he'd been artfully avoiding for forty-eight hours: Why had he nearly sacrificed everything to heat things up with her? And why was the suggested cooling off feeling like more of a punishment than a good idea? Surely he could focus on work and her. Why couldn't she manage Alix, then on her off time… His mouth went dry as he escaped once again into the memory of her curls spread against his chest. No, the distraction was devastating to his productivity, and if Alix, or anyone else for that matter, were to find out about their tryst, the consequences would be far reaching and expensive. Even for a Hartmann. Especially for this Hartmann.

Exhaling, he turned his attention to the email in front of him. It was a huge deal. China making a move in beef commodities.

"I need to talk to Daniels. Can you get Jeff on the phone?"

The directive shot her into action. "Of course, give me a moment."

The intercom on his desk buzzed. "Jeff Daniels on line one, and you're to return a call from Kellerman."

Nick clicked his phone to line one. "Nick, what can I do for you?" Jefferson was a family friend, issued from blue-chip stock.

"We need to chase Chinese dollars. With the new tariff strategy being announced, I want to see Hartmann beef with a bigger presence in Asia. Where are we with the joint venture proposal and the Shenghen brothers?"

"Things are good. Feng's jet touches down in two weeks, nothing a discreet gala couldn't firm up?" Jeff's voice trailed off.

"You want the brothers to come here?"

"Yeah. We can give them a Stetson, show them why Hartmann beef is the top end of the market and offer a Wild West you can taste in the brisket…"

"Look, I don't have time to host a party right now." Nick's tone reverted to his terse standard.

"As if you've got a huge part to play hosting any-thing. Call Josephine. She can pull together black-tie faster than most people can find their own underwear."

"All right. Have your team coordinate with Saman-tha. We'll do it." Nick smiled.

One down. Now to call the lawyer.

"I got your message. What can you tell me, Saul?"

There was a brief pause on the line. "It's not good, Nick. There's been an official petition for custody, an aunt apparently." Nick heard the shuffle of papers through the phone and set his jaw in grim determina-tion.

"There's a lot we can do. The fact there's a will, that you assumed custody directly and of course your brother's written directive—I wouldn't say it's a real threat." Saul spoke as though he were working through a bullet point list.

"My money-grubbing sister-in-law can't keep her nose out of it, is that it?" Nick felt his temper rise.

"Shouldn't be a problem—we're filing a counter-suit today. We'll right the ship." Saul didn't sound con-cerned, so hopefully the custody suit was nothing.

"Right, please keep me closely apprised." He discon-nected and made his way to the second living room. All the talk of Chinese beef and tariffs and the call with Saul had left his head buzzing. He longed to anchor his thoughts.

"You're confusing the armies again, love. The South was the Confederate Army, I'm pretty sure…"

From his position, leaning against the doorframe, he had a clear view of Mary flipping through a huge textbook. She lifted a finger to her mouth, licking it, then flipped another page, eyes scanning until she pushed her finger down and tapped it against a block of text. "See here? I was right." His stomach tightened at the sight of her pink tongue.

"You don't gotta sound so pleased with yourself, Mary. I can read, you know." Alix gave her tutor a good-natured shove, which Mary met with a smile.

"Darn right you can, you're a machine!" She smiled again, then, noticing him, colored pink.

"I'm gonna have to agree with Mary—you're definitely not an ordinary teenager." He smiled at Alix and, to his surprise, she smiled back. He accepted the smile as an invitation to join them, and sauntered in, taking a seat beside his niece. "So I had an interesting call today," he started.

"Tease," Alix accused.

He smiled. "Easy, I was just getting started." His hand snaked out and tousled her hair. "We're hosting a gala. A small one," he hurried to correct.

"Gala?" Mary mouthed the word, but no sound came out.

"Yep. I've got a new joint venture on the table, with a Chinese group, the Shenghen brothers." He was speaking to Alix, but looking at *her*. Hard not to as she was channeling her thousand-watt smile in his direction.

To hell with cooling off. He had to figure out a way to get the woman on a date. After hours, of course.

"Get to the gala already," Alix insisted. "What do

we wear? Will there be other teens there? Is it like a masked party or…" She was speaking rapidly, tripping over her words in the excitement over a soiree to break up the monotony of homeschooling.

Nick laughed and shook his head. "I'm afraid it's gonna disappoint you."

Alix snorted. "Not likely. I love parties." Her eyes shone with sincerity.

"Maybe we could find a way to help. Plan it, I mean. We could work it into a lesson. Make a budget, calculate returns, cost per serving. I'm sure I can think of something." Mary's tone matched Alix's, but her train of thought was interrupted with an ecstatic squeal.

"Yes! I want to—yes, yes, yes! We are gonna plan a sick party!" Alix jumped to her feet.

"Ah-ah-ah," Mary tutted. "Maybe this offers a lovely opportunity for a little research? Maybe we could write an essay on joint ventures? Or East Asian investment in the commodities market?"

"Mary, let's discuss how to make the gala a learning opportunity."

"I'd love that," she answered, eyes widening in his direction.

"I've got meetings until six. Maybe you can stop by. My room. After dinner," he finished.

"Yes, sir." She winked. "Anything for a gala."

Alix fell back onto the couch, busy on her phone. "We gotta have the most epic food. It's all about the Instagram opportunities now." She was muttering to herself, swiping wildly at her screen.

He was in for it. Both women were excited, and he

had somehow managed to hand over the largest business deal of his career to the naive fingers of his niece and her delicious tutor. Clearly, he also had a lot to learn; he just hoped the price of the ensuing education was palatable.

Twelve

Nick.

He could hear her. Taste her.

He wondered if his skin had some sort of memory, programmed to want her. He'd dreamed of her sneaking out of his bedroom again. He could have sworn his sheets still smelled like her. And he couldn't seem to stop thinking of her hair against his pillow, as arousing as the creamy velvet of her inner thighs.

He shook his head. This distraction was precisely why she'd been right about cooling things off. Seven generations of Hartmanns had run this ranch. He needed control of all his faculties if he was going to keep this land, and more if he was going to transform it. To expand the empire of their holdings, he needed more than control; he needed mastery of every faculty he had.

Doubling down on a newfound commitment to his goals, Nick was pulled back to the present. Lunch, here with Ben.

"Earth to Nick." Ben waved a beer stein in his direction.

"Right. Sorry." Nick shrugged.

"Nick, I can't hold her off any longer. This is going to happen. Best you just accept it." Ben's frustration coursed through his speech and beer licked over the edge of his glass as he placed it forcefully on the high-top table, front of house, at Chez Gregoire.

"I peeled myself away from the ranch for a front seat to your whine-fest?" Nick swallowed the last dregs from his own pint and ran a hand through his hair, pulling the loose strands from his face. "Snap out of it. Three weeks is nothing in the scheme of things." He was aware of the exasperation in his tone, but he couldn't be bothered to mask it.

"Three weeks of trying to convince Josephine she'd cause more stress than good by interceding? Talking the woman off a ledge on a moment's notice?"

"How bad is it?" Nick asked.

"Pretty bad. She won't stop calling—haven't you listened to any of her messages?" Ben hunched forward and lined up his cutlery in even parallel lines across his place mat. "Apparently you won't return her calls?"

"Oh, Benjamin, you're the son she always wanted." Nick laughed, but it was hollow. Ben's reputation for calling Josephine back minutes after any trace of a missed call was well-earned. To be fair, Ben had been a fixture around the Hartmann residence growing up, having lost his own mother at age eight. He'd latched onto Josephine and had never let go. One would think the discord in the Hartmann home would have dissuaded him, but no.

"You're lucky to have her. You should call her back." Ben had hackles up at the mere insinuation he went too far in his admiration of the Hartmann matriarch.

"Fine, you've made your point. I'll call her." Thankfully, the waiter arrived with refills, and as both men ordered the house special for lunch, the tension dissipated.

"You're quiet," Ben noticed.

"Lots on my mind." Nick reached for his glass and took another sip of his pale ale.

"Such as?"

"I've been playing a game of voice-mail tag of my own." He put his cell phone on the table, covering it with his hand. The damn thing was a curse. It gave the illusion of communication, but he was still the same victim to his sister's schedule.

Ben eyed the phone and raised an eyebrow.

"Evie. I've been trying to get ahold of her, but it's been a desert, communication-wise."

It was impossible to miss the twitch in Ben's jaw. They'd been best friends long enough for Nick to see through the charade of nonchalance his buddy put up when it came to his sister Evie. Sure, he didn't get the obsession, but he'd never kicked into that hornet's nest. It was a no-go zone in their friendship, probably the only one.

"That doesn't seem like her," was all Ben acknowledged.

The *salade Niçoise* arrived, and both men tucked in.

"I guess," Nick said through a mouthful of tuna, swallowing it down before continuing. "I guess she's a bit sore about the ranch. Pausing the sale, I mean." He knew he'd find an ally in that argument with his buddy.

"Yeah, well, I can't say I blame you. Hartmann Homestead's been in the family for ages."

"I guess her acting career wasn't the slam dunk she had hoped for," he added.

"I could fly out there, explain it to her, calm, like, you know, show her your point of view, maybe get her to call you back? Does she know about the Chinese interest you've drummed up? About the gala? There's a lot of opportunity here now."

This was going precisely the way Nick intended. "Aww, I couldn't ask you to do that," he said through a wide smile.

"No, really, I wouldn't mind. Stallion I've had my eye on is going to auction out west next week."

"I think if Evie would listen to anyone, it'd be you."

"Say no more, consider it done." Ben smiled. "You bringing a date to the gala?"

Nick shook his head. Satisfaction couldn't come close to describing the feeling washing over Nick in that moment. Evie was the last piece of his puzzle, and what he had said was true: if she'd listen to anyone, it would be Ben. As for a date? There was only one person he was interested in, but he wouldn't fall into that trap, despite his appetite.

Nick brushed his hand through his hair and pulled into the barn. Rowen, his favorite stallion, was saddled for him, waiting for a ride. He needed a moment of calm. A moment to reconnect. Then he'd tackle the problem he'd been putting off.

Once out of pasture, they settled into a relaxed gait, putting some distance between the house and themselves. Twenty minutes out, he tapped on his phone and touched his Bluetooth headphones. "Siri, call Mom."

He wasn't sure what he expected and smiled in surprise at her quick answer.

"Took you long enough," she said. A dutiful practitioner of call screening, Josephine Hartmann only answered when she felt like it. 'Course, it helped that she'd been trying to get in touch with him for three weeks.

"Sorry, Mom. Things have been a bit busy, you could say." Rowen's gait slowed, and the horse pulled down to snack on some dandelion. "Whoa, boy," he muttered under his breath, squeezing his thighs together.

"Excuse you?"

"I was talking to Rowen, sorry." He cleared his throat.

"Never thought I'd see the day my own son refused to call me back," she started to rant.

"I'd have thought you were used to it by now, what with Austin's allergy to family communication."

"Nice, Nicholas. Nice."

"Right, sorry. What did you want to chat about?" Best keep her on track, he figured.

"Maybe I wanted to know when would be a good time to see my only granddaughter? Or if my son would be open to dinner with a lovely daughter of a friend I met at bridge club? Could it be I want to talk about the ranch, and why the broker called me about the suspension in the listing?" She was talking without pause, and Nick rolled his eyes.

"I'm not looking for a date. Alix is handful enough, thanks." He clipped out his words, instantly regretting them. She wasn't a handful. She was a sad kid.

"You've heard, then? About the petition? That woman, Francesca, she called me, full of threats."

"She doesn't have a leg to stand on, Mom." The sun fell lower in the sky, and he pressed forward at a faster pace in an effort to leave the bugs behind him. The canter had him moving with the horse and it was easy to lose himself as the wind rushed past his ears.

"Don't be so sure. She mentioned a second will to me. A letter from her sister?"

Nick cursed. "I'll call Saul in the morning." Hopefully, it was nothing a little more money couldn't fix.

"I'm shocked I haven't been invited to visit. Didn't it occur to you that I might be able to help with the handful?" Josephine sniffed.

"Alix doesn't need a sitter, Mom, but you're more than welcome to come and boss around the household staff if you'd like."

"How about tomorrow, then?" She was to the point, which made the proposal tough to skirt.

"Yeah, fine. I can't wait." He disconnected and stared to the horizon.

A squeeze of his thighs, and Rowen picked up the pace, taking them down the path to his own thinking rock, miles from the house, from the blonde tutor he couldn't stop thinking about and the niece he'd never known he wanted but couldn't bear to lose.

Thirteen

Whatever it was, it wasn't good.

Her stomach had turned over the moment Alix passed the envelope to her, smug smile plastered to her face.

"I think this is meant for you?" To Rose, the girl's tone sounded accusatory.

She accepted the envelope, addressed to Miss Rose Kelly, and retreated double-time to her room. *That Ellen. Bloody instigator.* Only *her* relative would bother penning an actual letter in this digital age. Mary and Ellen were so similar in that vein that Rose couldn't hold the oddity against her cousin. She supposed it was a good thing her sis hadn't been more technological, or she wouldn't have been able to step into her life here in Montana.

The post had arrived moments into breakfast, but she'd lost her appetite when a gleam of curiosity regis-

tered on Alix's face. Nick hadn't been there; with the
gala imminent, he wasn't around much these days. Just
as well, it was becoming more and more difficult to
keep from remembering their one night together when
he entered a room.

Had Alix noticed?

Heaven. Could she not have twenty bloody minutes
without thinking about him?

She kicked her feet ahead of her and stretched on the
coverlet of the bed. The letter was cheery enough. She
scanned the page, the ordered penmanship easy to read,
and paused on the salient points of her note: *things are
fine at the flat, heaps of mail for you, scanning them to
your inbox. Included a pic of your pen pal, heaps more
letters here. I told you—you should have canceled.*

It was the type of message she could have sent via
text, but *no*, she'd had to address it to Rose Kelly and
mail it. At least it had been Alix giving her the letter
and not Nick himself, or worse, his conniving secretary.
Rose looked at the picture her cousin included. A kid
whose eye surgery she hoped to sponsor. She smiled
with a renewed determination to earn out this contract.

She pulled her leaden feet off the bed and answered
the quiet knock at her door, surprised to find her young
charge wringing her hands. Gone was the previously
smug mailwoman and before her was a fresh-faced
sixteen-year-old, stripped of all attitude. *What was up?*

"Alix, I thought we were meeting at nine?"

"Yeah, I know." The girl shifted from foot to foot.
Her hair, worn long, trailed past her shoulders and fell
in front of her face, an auburn curtain shielding her expression from closer inspection.

"Can I help you with something?" Rose opened the door wider.

"My grandma is coming tonight. Nick just told me." The girl stood, feet rooted in place, and cautiously looked up.

Perhaps Rose wasn't an Oxford-educated tutor, well, not any tutor at all for that matter, but she did have a knack for people, and she saw straight through the tough-girl act Alix often wore. "Why don't you come in, have a cuppa with me. I've got a cinnamon chai brewing, it's lovely."

"Sure, yeah, okay." Alix made her way to the over-size armchair beside the bed, and sank into it, punching back the pillow before wriggling into the duvet across her knees.

"Would you say you're close to your gran?" Rose poured a steady stream of freshly brewed tea into the second mug and offered it to her guest.

"Close?" Alix scoffed. "No, not close. I've met the woman, like, twice? I barely know any of the Hartmanns."

"What about your mom, Katherine? Did she have any family?" Rose was careful to keep her tone soft, and she purposefully avoided looking at Alix, instead focusing on the coverlet.

"My mom? Yeah. She has a sister. Francesca. I have a cousin I kinda know, Wendy. She didn't have to go to boarding school."

"Sure. You know, when I was a kid, I dreamed of going to boarding school. It's really cool in London, the old buildings, secret passageways. I used to wish my door was a swinging bookcase I could hide behind."

Rose was rewarded with a laugh from Alix.

"I was a bit worried that you don't have any mates around here," Rose continued, tapping a finger on the edge of the mug with nervous energy.

"Mates? You mean like friends?" She shook her head. "I didn't love boarding school. No hidden staircases or anything where they sent me." Alix smiled, but the smile was tight.

"If you didn't like boarding school, why were you there?" It was the question Rose had wanted most to ask.

"My parents. I wasn't exactly a planned baby. My mom never wanted kids. And when I turned eleven, I was sent to my first sleepaway school. Anyway, it's the same story I bet you've heard a lot of poor little rich kids tell." Alix was chewing on her lip.

"Right, well, you've got that behind you now." She didn't want to go into all the stories she *didn't* have. "I've always wanted a big family, but it was just my sister and me for as long as I can remember. I also have a cousin. She's pretty annoying."

Another laugh. Perfect. Rose took another sip of tea and continued. "I'd love to meet your gran. Do you think you want to…" Rose let her voice trail off, a classic trick she'd used time and time again behind the bar.

"To do what?" Alix brightened at the intrigue.

"I was thinking maybe a little makeover for tonight?" Rose smiled. If Alix were anything like her sixteen-year-old self, a makeover was a great plan.

"Like, a big makeover?" She spoke with cautious optimism. Rose knew when to seize a victory.

"Yeah, we need to elevate our looks, anyway, with a

posh gala only four days away. I was thinking, we pop into town—" she ventured a wink "—and maybe get a little update to our wardrobe? I've had two paydays pass and haven't spent a cent. I mean, I can't donate it *all*…"

"Yes. I'm totally into this idea." Alix now wore a wide smile and had jumped to her feet. "When are we leaving?"

"Let me have a chat with your uncle. I'll need to borrow a vehicle. How do you think we can spin this as educational?" Rose was now chewing on her own lip, eyes shining with a sense of shared rule-breaking. And because she had an excuse to get back in front of Nick.

"You're the tutor," Alix flipped back, skipping the few steps to the door. "Aren't you?" she added as a saucy afterthought.

"Right, yes, of course I am. I was just trying to decide if shopping was more tied to variable algebra or maybe, um, social studies. Give me a few minutes to read through some notes and get the okay from your uncle for a pair of keys."

How he had been talked into a girls' day out was still beyond him. He had a multimillion-dollar empire to run, an export offer to pull together, but here he was, driving the forty minutes into town, just because she had asked.

She. Alix. She. Mary. It didn't matter; he'd have taken the commute for either of them, and the two beauties knew it.

"So what is it exactly you're doing?" Country music filled the back seat of the car, and Alix was nodding her head to the beat of a song on her phone. Just as well, it gave him a chance to talk to *her*.

"Variable algebra, in a real-time setting. Makes it more approachable."

He laughed. "Do you think speaking in a posh accent validates your lesson plans? Just admit you wanted to shop." He rolled down the driver's-side window and let his arm lie relaxed on the outer edge of the car, allowing himself to wonder for a moment if perhaps she wanted to spend the afternoon with him as badly as he wanted to spend it with her.

They'd been cooling off for weeks now and somehow he was even hotter than before their night together. The cooling off wasn't working for him; if anything he wanted her more than ever.

"Shopping? It's Tuesday. This is a lesson plan," she insisted. She met his gaze and then licked her lips. The glimpse of her tongue left his body tight with desire.

"Quite the tutor you have yourself, Alix. I hope you appreciate her," he said over his shoulder, and the teen perked up with the comment.

In the passenger seat, Mary smiled, then ran a hand along her leg, slowly, deliberately, pulling the hem of her dress up. He was going to need more than a cold shower to dampen this inferno. She was playing with him and he knew it, but he didn't mind. He liked it.

"Sure, I love algebra now. Favorite course of mine, variable equations…all that." Her eyes sparkled and her animated reply provoked a grin from Nick.

"I'm clearly at your mercies, ladies." He laughed.

The easy chatter in the front seat had time flying by,

and before he was ready to let the womenfolk out of his sight they arrived downtown. He pulled in front of a high-end salon, and dropped the women off, promising to collect them in three hours for a lunch date. He could meet with Saul while they got the shopping out of their system.

"Take this, then." He offered a black credit card to Mary, but Alix swiped it before her fingers could close around it.

"Probably better if I manage the card? She's so British. Might be shocked by our comfort in propping up the local economy."

"Sure." He laughed. "Just be sure to get something black tie for you each—we've got the gala."

"Cool. Yes. Black tie. We are so in." Alix tucked the card into a Prada wallet and slipped the wallet into her purse before turning to Mary. "Coming?"

Nick slid the car into Park, and Alix hopped out.

"I'll join you in a moment," Mary called after her, getting out of the car herself. Her skirt fluttered in the wind, and Nick's breath caught at the long expanse of leg offered by the breeze. She caught his gaze, and played with the hem again just long enough to hypnotize him.

"Yes, you get started. I need to discuss something with Mary," Nick added, willing himself to look away from her legs.

Mary shook her head and took a step toward the store, but Nick hopped out of the car and motioned to the side street to the left of the store entrance. The sun shone hot on the back of his neck, and to his relief, she followed him to privacy.

"I had an idea…" With a few steps more, he moved into her space, nearly pressing her against the brick facade of the building. He wanted more, needed more, and he hoped she did, too. He was about to find out.

"Someone could see us," she hissed.

"In the alley? At nine thirty on a Tuesday? No, we have a few minutes." His hands ran down over her body, exploring the sweep where her thigh joined her ass in a glorious curve. She widened her stance, welcoming him.

"You left before I had my breakfast," he accused. "Are you still wanting things to stay cool between us? I'm hungry…"

She shook her head, and his mouth covered hers with expert efficiency. One finger pushed against the elastic of her panties, and she let her head fall back against the wall.

"I want you, Mary." The woman was addictive, and he was pretty sure she knew it.

"Not in the alley. Tonight," she managed in a ragged breath.

She wanted him, too. A fierce longing swept through him at her response.

He covered her mouth again. She melted into him, meeting every parry of his tongue, and pressing her chest against his.

She twisted and was free of his grasp with a quick twirl. She took another step out of the shadows, before turning and looking at him. With a slow deliberation, she put her hands under her skirt. Shimmying, she stepped out of a cotton lavender thong. "Why don't you hang on to these for me?"

A few steps and she was back in front of him, and while he was too shocked to move, she tucked the small scrap of fabric into his back pocket. "Tonight, cowboy," she promised.

When she suggested a makeover, she hadn't meant a *Pretty Woman* moment, but Alix was clearly in her comfort zone shopping with a black credit card.

Rose turned to find Alix laden with a variety of dresses. "I—I can't possibly try on all that," she stammered, especially since she was now shy a pair of knickers thanks to her class act in the alley. She backed up toward the door.

"Oh, no, you don't. I wouldn't be a good friend if I didn't insist you try on that dress." Alix pointed at the gown at the back of the shop, and Rose flushed.

"That's the spring collection, the nicest couture in town." The sales associate perked up, clearly encouraged at the prospect of hitting her sales quota for the month with one sale.

But it wasn't the silk dress that had driven Rose's heart into her throat. *I wouldn't be a good friend if I didn't insist you try on that dress.* A very small corner of Rose felt a rush of pride. She and Alix were connecting. "Right. I'll try it on, but no promises."

Moments later, she peeled back her thin cardigan. The dress was quite something.

"How is it?" Alix was calling through the velour curtains, her voice dampened by the thick fabric.

How was it? The silk clung to her body, the sheen of the fabric reflecting light in all the right places. The silk, as light as butterfly kisses against her skin, was an inky blue so dark she had thought it black until a twist to inspect her rear offered a quick glimmer of navy. The cut? Designer. Rose was far from a fashion victim, but even to her untrained eye, she could tell the dress was expensive. Classy. Effortlessly sexy.

Everything she wanted to be when she saw Nick tonight.

"I'm coming in," Alix pronounced. "Wowza." She stopped after pulling back the curtain. Her bravado vanished, and she looked up at Rose, insisting, "You're, like, really beautiful. For serious."

It was difficult not to smile at the pronouncement, and instead of denying the compliment, she accepted it. "I guess I have to buy it."

"My uncle is going to love it," Alix answered, pulling the curtain closed before Rose could confirm or object to the knowing wink she heard in Alix's words.

The price tag fluttered as she rehung the dress on the wooden hanger. The dress was nearly two thousand dollars. For a slip of silk. Taking it off, she broke the spell of insanity.

"It's lovely, Alix, but I can't accept this dress from your uncle. I'm sure he didn't mean—"

"If you're trying to talk yourself out of that dress, forget it." Alix whipped back the curtain, rings sliding, and snatched the dress from the hook, dashing off.

"Excuse you?" Rose howled after her, tripping out of the dressing room before bothering to fasten her cardigan. Alix was already at the cash register.

Rose slapped her own credit card down on the counter. "I'll pay for this, Alix," she said.

For a moment, she didn't feel a twinge of regret at the largest purchase of her life, and instead felt only excitement. *Her friend* loved it. *Her friend's uncle* would love it, too. And the private tutor gig did pay pretty decently. She could afford the dress and the surgery sponsorship as long as she managed her other expenses.

Alix stared a moment at the Visa card, eyes widening, then stepped back from the counter. "If you're gonna insist, but it's no big deal. You've seen the ranch. I mean, this dress is a blip on the radar for us." She snapped her fingers to emphasize the fleeting effect the purchase would have on their bills.

Rose faced her charge and doubled down. "Sometimes, the dress means more if you buy it yourself. Plus, each time I pay down this outrageous bill, I'm gonna think of you."

The assistant picked up her card and slipped it through the machine. A moment too late, Rose realized the pause on Alix's face might have meant she had read the credit card name holder: *Rose Kelly.*

Fourteen

The lawyer was talking, but Nick wasn't listening. All he could think about was the alley. The brick wall. The woman who had rocked his world with a scrap of fabric. The thong burned a hole in his pocket and in his mind. That was the problem with Mary. She was unpredictable. He had to stop thinking about her, focus on the lawyer. On the ranch. Which he would do, after tonight.

"You see, you have nothing to worry about. Any petition Francesca can offer we can overcome, particularly with your mother's endorsement." Saul was nodding as he spoke, and with great effort Nick dragged his attention back to the task at hand: Alix.

"Great. So we're all set, then?" He flexed his fingers and tapped them on his thigh.

"For now, there's nothing more we can do. You're

the proxy, and it's been validated by the federal court.
The vote is yours until she's of age, that is to say the
next two general assemblies."

A two-year clemency. He could get her to fall in love
with the ranch in two years, especially if he managed
to avoid falling himself. He just had to keep his eye on
the endgame.

"Thanks. That sounds great." Nick rose and left,
eager to return to his role as chauffeur.

If there had ever been a doubt Alix was a Hartmann,
it was put to rest today. Per her text, the girls were waiting at an ice cream parlor; both were laden with shopping bags and finishing a frozen yogurt each.

He waited in the truck, observing a few moments
before waving to greet them.

"Nick, you're not gonna believe what we got for Sat-
urday." Alix was jabbering before even entering the
truck.

"Really, your niece has such lovely taste—the girl
could be a fashion designer herself," Mary added for
good measure. Then she looked up at him and while
maintaining eye contact recrossed her legs. His breath
caught in his throat.

She bit her lip, and he swallowed. Addictive indeed.

Bags deposited in the back, Mary opened the passenger door and scooted into the front seat. She had a
new shade of azalea pink lipstick, and it matched the
pink hue flushed to her cheeks.

"It's easy to pick out nice outfits when you look like
a model," Alix flipped back.

The kid was right about one thing: Mary Kelly was model material. He swallowed, wondering what she had picked up at the lingerie store. Immediately, he questioned the importance of this dinner tonight, figuring he could subside easily on a hearty round of dessert.

The forty-minute drive back to the ranch passed in a flash as both women regaled Nick with tales of their shopping, coffee date and their mishap in the shoe store. Mary, sitting in the front seat, kicked off her shoes and put her feet up on the dashboard.

"That's dangerous," Alix complained.

"You know me, I like to live dangerously from time to time."

Nick could swear she was talking only to him. Her skirt slid up her thigh, struggling to find purchase. He could almost see—

"...tons of stuff," Alix jabbered on from the back seat, launching into a recap of everything she'd tried on and bought.

He didn't say anything, just eyed Mary. She shook her leg, the movement causing her skirt to slide. He couldn't look away.

"Watch the road," she teased.

He managed to keep his eyes on the road the rest of the way, with willpower he hadn't known he possessed. The sun was high in the sky as the crew arrived back at the house.

"What's your plan for this afternoon?" Nick ventured.

"Fashion show?" Alix suggested hopefully.

"Not on your life. We gotta do a bit of work today," Mary interrupted.

"So you didn't manage as much variable algebra as you had hoped on your excursion?" Nick couldn't help himself.

Mary blushed. "Not as much as I had hoped."

"Speak for yourself," Alix added under her breath.

Nick opened the door, and stood back, letting the women pass ahead of him. He hesitated before making his way left, back to the home office. "Don't forget, my mom is coming tonight."

Alix was skipping down the hall, but to her credit, she paused and yelled, "Yeah, sure, we'll be there," over her shoulder.

With Alix out of the room, Mary held out her hand. "You can give them back now." She flushed.

He smiled. "Not likely."

"Come on, Nick. I was just joking around earlier."

"Don't try and hide it in a joke." He lifted a finger to his lips. "Shh, let's just talk about what you're wearing tonight."

"Just give them back." She held her hand out.

He caught her hand and raised it to his lips, pressing a kiss to her wrist. He could feel her pulse quicken, and decided to press his advantage. "Tonight, be naked under your dress."

He left before she could answer.

Back at his desk, Nick started going through a barrage of emails, but he kept wondering what his mom would think of the new tutor. How would he handle the two women alone? He might need some backup.

"Buddy?"

"I'm on my way," Ben answered before even being invited.

"How did you—"

"Jo called me. She wanted to know what to bring as gifts for Alix and her tutor."

"The tutor? Ah, Ben, what did you say to my mom?" Nick spun on his chair and ran a hand through his hair. Just what he needed…

True to his word, Ben arrived not long after their call, spit-polished and ready for a night with the matriarch. Nick made a mental note to buy a nice bottle of Scotch for his friend. First, dealing with Evie; now, taking on his mom? Nick struggled with the thought that perhaps he'd been a bit selfish lately when it came to his friendships. As soon as the gala and the custody battle were behind him, he was going to up his game as a committed wingman.

Josephine Hartmann was the picture of elegance. She was sixty-five but didn't look a day over fifty. A credit to her stylist, a disciplined habit of drinking eight glasses of water a day, never smoking and a sharp tendency to only buy clothes cut for her figure. She arrived promptly at six, entering the ranch after an awkward knock was left hanging in the air.

He rushed to the door, offering a hand to take his mom's coat as she breezed in, pecking an air-kiss to each of his cheeks.

"Where is she, then, darling?" The tone was arid and

cool. His mom had a way of keeping him and his siblings on their toes, and despite himself, a wave of guilt rushed through him.

"I'm sorry, Mom. I should have told you, but I've just been feeling a bit…" His voice trailed off when his mom put a cool hand on his arm.

"It's a lot, son. All this. It's a lot. Stop putting so much pressure on yourself. You're doing a good thing. But try to remember, I'm on your side through all this. I support you, my dear, *most* of the time." She gave a quick squeeze and lifted her chin. "So? Where is she?"

Nick led the way to the living room, where Ben was entertaining the women. Chesapeake furniture featuring heavily carved wooden elements scattered the room under cashmere plaids and large down pillows, and a cheery fire in a ten-foot-wide fireplace threw a gold cast over the room. Alix and Mary stood together facing the fire, backs to them. Alix had a hand snaked around Mary's waist, and the two stood in static stillness entranced by the flames.

Mary's hair, lush ringlets, fell just past her shoulders, worn loose. Nick cleared his throat and both women spun to face him. She wore a butter-yellow sundress with a Peter Pan collar. It wasn't a sexy cut, but from the blush on her face he guessed at her nakedness underneath and determined he'd never seen a hotter ensemble.

"Mary, Alix, I'd like you to meet Josephine, the official head of the family." He stepped forward to present his mom.

Josephine and Alix stood like two dogs, sizing each

other up. Alix, breaking first, lowered her head, and his mom took a step forward in answer.

"Alix, I've waited quite a long time to see you," Josephine began.

"Not like it was much of a mystery where I was," Alix answered.

"Alix." Mary beat him to the punch, a quick rebuke, delivered with hawklike precision.

"Sorry," Alix mumbled under her breath. "I just meant, if she'd really wanted to know me, she hardly needed to wait until my parents died."

"Nick was telling me things are going better with Francesca?" Ben offered in a bid to interrupt and lighten the mood.

"Aunt Fran?" Alix perked up.

"Well, it seems there's a second claim on your guardianship. Nothing we can't sort out, Alix, so don't worry about it." Nick threw a dagger with his eyes and Ben smiled sheepishly.

The mention of Francesca added a thick layer of tension to the room, and Nick fidgeted. "So, I think Pierre has quite the spread waiting for us. Anyone hungry?" Sure, they generally started evenings like this with drinks, but he figured liquid courage was not the answer to tonight's tension.

"So early?" His mom raised an eyebrow, but in lieu of an answer, Nick marched the troupe toward the dining room.

The dining room was lit by over fifty candles, and the room basked in the same gold glow that had met them in the living room. Sure, there was no fireplace, but they didn't miss it for all the splendor of the room.

"Lovely," Mary whispered as they rounded the corner.

Josephine took her habitual seat at the head of the table, and Nick sat to her right, Alix opposite. "Sit here," Nick invited, drawing the chair next to him out a few feet.

With dessert came the inquisition. *At least they made it past the main course.*

"Your sister has been calling quite a bit," his mother started. Nick noticed that Alix leaned forward, nosy kid.

"Well, Evie isn't too pleased with me at the moment."

"And why wouldn't she be pleased?" his mother asked, as though she didn't already know, an irritating quality that brought him right back to his childhood.

"I've a feeling you've got a good idea." He shot a glance at Alix, who was working on her pie as though it had wronged her in some way, jabbing to spear each chunk of apple.

"You've delisted the ranch," his mom added.

"I hardly think now's a good time to discuss it." Typical Josephine, everything was on her agenda and timeline.

"If you'd answer my calls, we could have discussed it earlier. For now, I'd like to know why you're going against your siblings' wishes?"

Beside him, Mary sputtered some of her drink.

"My job is to make decisions. Dad saw to that. Perhaps Austin wanted to sell, sure, but this ranch is our heritage, and now Alix can make that decision herself."

He looked at her and smiled and, for once, she met his gaze directly.

"Convenient, then, isn't it?" His mom couldn't help herself.

"Convenient?" He didn't bother veiling his tone. This was thin ice. "As her guardian, I'm in a position to help make decisions to best preserve her interest until she comes of age."

"Such as cloistering her here, away from any counter-opinions? Away from her education?" Josephine's regal facade slipped for a minute, and her forehead betrayed her emotions with a few lines screwing up in anger.

"Away from her education? I hired the best tutor money could buy. She's being educated by a pro, and I'll not apologize for it." He threw his hands down on the table. "Now can we enjoy our dessert or not?" He glowered at his mother.

Josephine eyed Mary, a fresh victim for her inquisition. "Nick tells me you're an Oxford graduate? Top of your class? What made you want to be a tutor?" It was the first question Josephine had directed toward Mary all evening, and Nick could feel the tension roil in the woman to his right.

"Yes, right, Oxford. Yes, it was a brilliant school."

"Sure is. Only the best for our Alix, right?" This time, the question was directed to Nick, who, in lieu of an answer, just nodded his assent.

"Do you find Montana living up to your hopes? As the top graduate, I was wondering why you'd choose to come here rather than Dubai or maybe Singapore. I know in-demand tutors with a wide-spectrum curriculum capability are heavily recruited."

Mary forked a piece of pie, and pointed to her chewing mouth, taking a moment to swallow before answering. She took a sip of water, then ventured a cautious, "I love Montana actually." Her cheeks pinked, and she added, "You know, I had no appetite for a haughty sheikh or oil baron's child. I became a tutor to make a difference. It's been important to me since my own parents passed away."

In the candlelit room, Nick noticed a softening around his mother's mouth and smiled. Amazing, Mary had even thawed his mother.

Mary continued. "I got the call with the job offer, and my answer came on autopilot. I like to feel needed." She looked down at her hands, twisted in her lap, and before he could stop himself, Nick reached under the table to take one in his. Her hand was small in his. Then, suddenly, her thumb pressed over the crest of his hand. If she was feeling for his pulse, the quickening would be impossible to ignore. As it stood, he didn't even try to hide it.

She made no eye contact with him, and just continued to stroke his hand under the table.

"More wine, anyone?" Nick offered, feeling a second wind of energy overcome him.

"Definitely." Ben pushed a glass forward, as though a strong dousing of alcohol could salvage the night.

"I'm glad you're not in Dubai." It was Alix, eyes shining, who spoke.

"Yes, indeed," Josephine added, and from the corner of his eye, he saw the small smile spread across her face.

"Me, too," Mary added.

"Me three," Nick finished.

All in all, it was a pretty smooth evening. She was the spoonful of sugar everyone needed; albeit a peculiar tutor, she was the perfect fit. He squeezed her hand again and felt the reassuring squeeze back.

He could barely wait to get her alone, and was driven to distraction with the wait. With the want.

Rose wasn't sure what she'd been expecting. She hopped up on her bed, head spinning from the evening's dinner. What had his mom thought of her? He'd taken her hand, unprompted. That wasn't sexual, but it sure felt intimate. Her head hurt from trying to make sense of it all.

She nearly missed the soft knock. Without the hushed, "Mary, it's me, are you awake?" she mightn't have answered.

"Nick?" She opened the door, revealing her favorite cowboy dressed in a relaxed T-shirt and snug jeans.

"Is it later yet?"

"I sure hope so."

"Did you want a nightcap?" he asked.

Would she like a nightcap with him? Damn right she did. "Lemme just grab a shawl." She turned and made for her bathroom, spritzing another shot of perfume in passage.

Such was how they ended up back in front of the fire, in his office.

"Whiskey?" he asked as he poured one for himself at the wet bar. The floor-to-ceiling wood paneling, over-size leather furniture and ten-foot-high wall of leather-bound books in his office would leave the set designer from *Beauty and the Beast* envious and inspired.

"Yes, of course," she answered.

He brought the two drinks with him as he joined her on the sofa. "So now you've met my mom," he ventured.

"Sure did, she's lovely."

"You're lovely." He reached a hand to tuck a stray curl behind her ear. "Your hair is like spun gold," he said softly, and pulled at another curl, watching it spring back into place. "I've wanted to touch it all evening. Touch *you* all evening. Every day since we left Jacks's rodeo."

"Are you hitting on an employee, *sir*?" She smiled back. *Please keep going.*

A shadow of indecision flickered across his face. She wasn't the only one who knew they were skirting close to a very blurry line. But he clicked his glass against hers and vanquished his doubts. "I am. I *so* am." He lifted his glass in cheers.

She sank closer to him on the couch, drawn magnetically. For a few minutes, they sat in silence, basking in the glow from the fire, focused on the heat between their touching bodies.

"I'm glad you're not in Dubai," he added. His hair, a mess of long dark locks, reached his shoulders. She pressed her eyes shut. The man had her dreaming of the things he could do to her.

"I'm glad, too." She swallowed, licking her lips, her tongue acting of its own accord.

"You know full well what you're doing to me," he said matter-of-factly, sipping his whiskey as he studied her.

"Do I?"

"Don't you?"

She leaned into the question, crossing into his space again. He smelled divinely masculine. Like the woods.

She had been so good. She had tried to cool things off, but the yearning persisted. And now, she was connecting with Alix, fulfilling her sister's dreams… She deserved this. She nudged closer to him and parted her lips.

"Mary." He kissed her. Hot, and full of promise.

She pulled away. "Don't talk." The last thing she wanted to be right now was Mary.

His hands, on a mission to torture her, pushed her against the back of the couch, the leather a cool contrast to the wet heat spreading through her.

"Your wish is my command."

As he kissed her, he touched her, trailing fingers over her arms, up her legs, pausing at the buttons at the back of her dress. "Off. I want this off." He fiddled with the small buttons, which seemed even smaller against his large fingers.

She didn't answer, just stood and made quick work of unbuttoning her dress. She hadn't planned this—why hadn't she planned this? She'd known she'd finish here, well, not here per se, but with him, naked. Her lack of planning with her wardrobe resulted in a thin white cotton bra, no underpadding, no underwire even, just a simple white brassiere. Against her pale skin, it seemed wholly inadequate for this rancher CEO. She should be in Agent Provocateur or some other fancy lingerie. The top of her dress fell to her waist, held in place by a belt. She brought both hands to cover her in a flash of modesty. She wasn't wearing any underwear, on his orders. He whistled, pushed up from the sofa and took a step closer to her, then another, until there was no space between them.

He pressed a kiss into her neck, and another in a hot trail to her ear.

"Have I told you, Ms. Kelly, I find you devastating?"

She smiled.

"Devastatingly attractive, my God. It feels religious, being here with you now." Another hot kiss, this time aimed lower, his mouth trailed over the thin cotton of her bra before tucking the fabric beneath her breast and feasting on the treasures beneath.

"Nick." She managed a strangled cry of his name and squirmed beneath him. "I want to touch you." She pulled his shirt over his head. Hot ridges of muscle begged to be touched and she marveled at his physique. Damn. It didn't get old, this sight. Her fingers followed every ridge, starting with the hard chest and moving down, tracing his abs, and swirling in the light sprinkle of hair that dipped into his waistband.

"Let's go." He broke away, his hand flying to his belt, pausing her exploration.

"Go? Not likely, Nick. I'm just getting started." Gone were her inhibitions; she was buzzing with attraction.

She'd fallen.

Who knew how much longer she'd live in this fairy tale before her karmic bill came due?

"I'm hardly going to ravish you on this couch." His delivery held little conviction, and with her one free hand, she managed to unhook the buckle of his belt.

His jeans slid away. He was hot against her, and she leaned into him, pulling him closer. "I want to feel you," she said, biting down on the bump of muscle on his shoulder.

"Did you spend the day bare?" he asked, catching her hand in his.

"Wouldn't you like to know?" She flirted back, bringing her hands back to his chest.

"Yes, very much." He lifted the hem of her dress. She felt his rough fingers explore her, taking in the satisfied look in his eye when he stroked her, no barrier between them. "Good girl," he crooned.

"Sometimes." She kissed him, finishing with a nip to his lower lip.

"Go to bed with a vixen, don't be surprised if you get bit, is that it?"

"I don't see a bed here." She bit him again.

"You're too sexy for your own good." He gripped her head, tangling a hand in her curls.

"What about your own good?" She pressed a kiss on his chest, and looked up.

"My welfare would be greatly aided by a little less talking and a little more loving."

She shuddered. Loving. The word slipped out, innocuous and unassuming on his lips, but she couldn't ignore it. It was too close to being real, even if he hadn't meant it that way. It was the difference between smiling and laughing. Of loving and sex. Right now, she'd happily smile if it was with him. But not more. *More* was not something she knew how to do. The correction was necessary. "They don't call this loving back where I come from."

Frowning, she tightened her lips. She couldn't lose herself, not while she had so much on the line. But maybe she could smile and mean it. Lord knew she wanted to.

"Well, maybe you've been doing it wrong." He grinned. "Come, let's go to my room. Spend the night with me." He kissed her, and she felt herself smile against his lips. "The whole night."

She wanted to. With everything that she was. To not have to wake up and sneak away as she had at the rodeo. But no. She could sleep with him, but men you fell asleep with? They meant trouble.

"Sounds like a good way to get hurt." She was surprised she'd said it aloud. She hadn't meant to. His hands stilled, and he brought a single finger to her chin, tilting it toward him.

"Well, I couldn't have that now, could I? You're right, let's stick to—"

"What was it I said before? You talk too much." She couldn't bear to have him belittle what they had. They weren't friends, and she didn't want to be a benefit.

"Maybe you should talk. Tell me what you want."

She looked at him and felt a pang in her chest. "I want to taste you," she admitted.

"Where?" His voice was rough.

"You know where." She took a step forward, gripping him. The pulsating heat was a lit match to the fire inside her. He twitched in her hand.

"What do you want?" he asked. She felt his hand on her arm, a gentle pressure as she sank to her knees.

"I want you inside me. Fast. Hard. I don't want it to stop until..."

"Until what?" He sank to the couch nearby and she scooted forward maintaining her proximity.

"Until I explode."

She didn't wait for a follow-up question, instead taking him in her mouth. It wasn't something she usually liked to do. But now? There was something undeniably erotic, feeling his hardness with her tongue. Knowing he wouldn't move. His hands went to her hair, pulling, tightening in her curls. It hurt a little, a sharp pain she liked, driving her tempo forward. One hand moved on his shaft, the other caressed his muscled thighs. He was so innately male. She felt a flexing tremble in his thigh and doubled her efforts. At this moment he'd surrendered to her. He was hers, but that surrender had a cost—her own surrender in kind.

"Enough," he breathed through gritted teeth.

She had no intention of stopping and didn't slow. He was close and she knew it. Then a strong hand stopped her.

"Vixen," he panted, before kissing her.

She bit him again, but just lightly. "What are you going to do about it?"

She could see the smile. Feel it as he covered her in

wide kisses. Feasting on her chest, her nipples tightening as he consumed them. Consumed her.

He took her then, without prelude or discussion. Her slick need for him was all the further encouragement required. He woke in her a selfishness she'd missed. A selfishness she only dreamed of but had never known. Gone was the concept of waiting, to explode together. Instead, she cried out on her own, melting in a chorus of sharp delight. But he didn't stop, just fueled her to spiral higher, reaching new heights. He paused before he came, endearments on his lips. He spoke with a reverence she wondered at.

Was she imagining it? It felt perfect.

"Tell me something no one else knows about you," she asked from her new vantage point on the rug by a dying fire.

"What do you want to know?" He trailed a finger over her ribs, lazy and without purpose. Just to touch her, she supposed. It didn't matter, she liked it.

"Tell me…" She paused. "Tell me why you're fighting so hard for this ranch."

His finger stilled.

"You never mention your dad. Is that part of it?"

"It's always part of it, isn't it?" His voice was quiet and she turned to look at him.

It was her turn, and she trailed a finger on him now, as though touching him would make it easier to talk.

"My mom said it was never about me. When he left."

"Your dad left?" she clarified. The revelation was new.

"For seven years. To find himself." Nick swallowed

hard. "I was fifteen. Twenty-two when he came back. But he missed the better part of Jackson's adolescence. Not to mention the girls'. Who knows, maybe Austin wouldn't have been such a jackass if he hadn't shouldered all that..." His voice trailed off.

"And?" She kept her voice small on purpose. As though a louder intonation would scare away his confessions. He rolled toward her and kissed her softly.

"I guess he left for him, and came back for us. When he left, I swore I'd be the man this ranch needed. The man our family needed. Austin never cared about the ranch, or admired Dad. I've learned to put the ranch first, always. I've made a lot of mistakes, but I'm gonna keep this land."

She nuzzled against him, and watched as the dying embers turned to ash. It was hard not to wonder if she counted as one of his mistakes.

Fifteen

"**D**amn thing's not cooperating," he muttered as he fiddled with his tie.

Maybe it was the sight of the sumptuous couch, where only four days ago he'd experienced nirvana, pressed against the supple leather with his British minx. They hadn't discussed it. Hadn't so much as mentioned the tryst, or the revelations following. She was infuriatingly distant, escaping with Alix at every opportunity, sequestering them both in the kitchen for hour-long chats with the chef about the costs of different menu items. Sure, he understood the need to make lessons relatable, but the avoidance was a tad extreme.

His phone buzzed. "Nick here," he answered, glad to set his maddening tie aside.

"Hey, it's Jeff. They arrive in Bozeman just shy of thirty minutes."

Thirty minutes, plus forty more for the drive, so he had about an hour to pull everything together. "Thanks, Jeff, you arriving on time?" He balled up his tie and chucked it away. The slip of fabric vivid on his bland desk.

"Sure am, not missing a Hartmann party. Not enough of them to look forward to as it is."

"Right, then, see you at seven." He hung up and Samantha breezed in. "Saul's office called, and he emailed over this will. I guess Fran's lawyer sent it." She handed him the fax and pursed her lips. "Let me just..." She took another step closer to him, snaked the tie off his desk and looped it around his neck.

"Er." He straightened.

"Lemme just," she whispered, leaning forward, tying his tie. Another step into his space. He stiffened. Somehow it felt wrong, the intrusion.

"Listen, Samantha, can you schedule a time for us to chat? I'd like someone I can trust at the head office. High time you were promoted."

She nodded, expression impossible to read.

He reached for the printed email. A second will, apparently Katherine's. Naming Francesca as Alix's guardian.

"For all we know, Francesca wrote this herself. Make sure no one sees this tonight."

Taking his dismissive tone as the cue it was, she spun on her heels and left without acknowledging the promotion. Just as well. Sure, it was true, with all the work she'd taken on after Austin's death, she might be due a raise, but how could he give it to her without giving her the wrong idea? He resolved to ask Ben, and made a mental note to bring it up the next time he saw him.

The sky was summer bright, and at six thirty, the cool of night had not yet fallen. The ranch was transformed. Josephine and Rebecca, the staff events coordinator, had outdone themselves once again, and the lawns were lit with thousands of candles, each encased in a handblown glass dome and suspended from random branches along the mile-long winding driveway.

The west wing of the ranch was similarly bedazzled. A staff of forty waiters, dressed in matching black uniforms, waited with limitless glasses of sparkling wine and champagne. Platters of canapés and mini deconstructed ribs along with other modern interpretations of classic American foods circulated among the guests.

"Anyone seen Ben?" he asked a passing waiter dressed with a blazer atop his fitted shirt, a team leader. He'd said Ben, but he'd meant Mary. Her name was always on the tip of his tongue, always top of mind.

"No, sir."

Just as well. He saw dozens of people he needed to meet with, starting with the mayor of Bozeman. He assessed the room before entering, then his eyes focused on her. Sakes alive, she was a stunner. A vision, really. Her curls piled atop her head, a messy spill of blond, the smell alive in his memory. He wondered if she smelled like lavender tonight. Her dress was simple, a blue-black silk that clung to her curves. Impossibly thin straps held up the sweetheart neckline, and the dress fell to the floor with a designer's considered simplicity. She leaned back, tilting her head, and laughed. The movement carried a leg forward and he swallowed. A white thigh pushed through a sky-high slit in the front of the gown. He felt a tightening in his body, an anticipation of what it might be like to run a hand across that leg, following it higher to its apex. He needed to get her out of here, somewhere alone, now.

Making a beeline toward her, he distracted himself in an effort to cool his body, focusing on her entourage—namely, the two Chinese men she was charming. No. The Shenghen brothers? Like moths to a flame, they were attracted to her because…well, because of course they were.

She was like the moon, and had a similar gravitational pull on him. He stopped for a moment. That was it. He had fallen for her. Like gravity. He couldn't fight it. He watched her work the room and it occurred to him, maybe she was the missing piece he needed. Maybe she would stay and be the partner he'd never had. One he deeply wanted.

"You lot are too much." Rose smiled, aware of the importance of her company.

"Ms. Kelly, it is you who are too much." Both men spoke with a trace of a British accent, and flirting with them felt somehow familiar.

She tilted her head back, smiling wider. "I'm afraid you're a bunch of flatterers, the lot of you." She reached for an arm and gave it a squeeze. Gazillionaires or not, men were men, and Rose was strangely in her element.

She had arrived before the first guest, flanked by her charge. She and Alix had made a tour of the party, both a tad gobsmacked by the glamorous transformation of the ballroom. Sure, to her, it had been glamorous to start with—the floor-to-ceiling windows gave way to a view unparalleled by any Rose had seen in her life. But after Rebecca was through with it? The same glass balls suspended from the fruit trees outside were suspended from the ceiling, in sweeping arcs of artistry casting the soft light of a thousand candles through the room. Chandeliers were lowered to create an ambience of comfortable intimacy, and the yellow light reflected off the many bedazzled dresses of the guests. Oversize bouquets of flowers six feet across released heady perfumes of jasmine and lily. The room was the picture of opulence and even her rich-kid student was silenced.

The ballroom was now invaded by glitterati, celebs flying in from both coasts, from top bankers to a rapper Alix idolized; the amalgamation of guests was the who's who of the society pages. The "small gathering" now welcomed at least two hundred people.

Nick's mother, dressed in an Egyptian-inspired chiffon dress, was pretty as a peach. Alix stiffened upon seeing her.

"Your dress is rather loud." Josephine's eyebrow shot up as she took in the hot-pink ensemble on her granddaughter.

"Thanks," Alix said, deliberate in her misinterpretation of the comment.

"I didn't mean it as a—"

"It's lovely to see you again, Mrs. Hartmann," Rose

cut in. She put on her best smile, retucking a stubborn curl behind her ear.

Josephine snaked a glass of champagne off a passing tray. "You look—" she paused and cast her eyes in a deliberate once-over of Rose "—presentable."

The matriarch spat out *presentable* in a tone that left it sounding like an insult, but Rose was British. Polite insults had been bred into her people for generations. "As do you." She smiled back.

"Did you check on the canapés?" Alix broke the tension with her question.

"Canapés? There's a caterer—I'm sure everything is to the Hartmann standard." Josephine arched her eyebrow again and beckoned a waiter to her side, replacing her now empty glass with a full one.

"Maybe we should check," Alix said.

Rose nodded. *Canapés* was their safe word, and she had committed to getting Alix out of any situation that would necessitate its use.

Once out of earshot, they huddled behind the four-piece jazz band. "She's the worst," Alix hissed.

"That's maybe a bit harsh," Rose interjected.

"You look presentable." Alix mimicked her gran with a fair copy and the two giggled.

Rose saw two men speaking in what Alix's research had proposed was likely Mandarin to a small group just as an aide came in their direction.

"Mr. Shenghen." She bowed into a deep curtsy.

"No, I'm his aide, but he'd like to meet you."

He'd like to meet you. In this dress, she believed it.

A huge part of her wanted to turn and run, but this was a massive business opportunity for Nick. For the ranch.

"With pleasure." She followed the aide and quickly found herself engaged in questions from the elder of the two brothers.

"Still fresh from the UK, I presume, as I don't hear a trace of the Western accent quite yet," he commented. But gone were her witty answers.

She saw Nick, towering a few inches over the heads of most of the crowd. No man had a right to look that good. He stood suave, confident and sexy as all hell. Once his eyes caught hers, they narrowed, and he made his way over to them.

Swallowing, she bit her lip.

She robotically nodded in reply, adding an obliging, "Yes, indeed."

"Feng, Liu." Nick's voice interrupted them and the men fell into a rapid succession of handshakes.

"Your tutor has been enthralling us with stories of the Wild West," Liu Shenghen started.

"Has she now?" Nick moved closer to her, and she took a step back, foot hitting the edge of the wainscoting. She'd reached a wall, both literally and figuratively.

"You're from the same stock. She's an Oxford grad, did she mention?" Nick smiled, an invitation to pick up the ball and run with it.

Of course she'd landed at the one ranch in Montana that would host a black-tie event with renowned alumni from her fake alma mater. Because that was her life. *Rose's life.* But now? Her ruse was important, to save face for Nick.

The brothers had graduated with honors from the business program, and they had a volley of questions. "What did you study? Did you board? Wasn't the library wonderful?"

"Easy, gentleman." She laughed in an effort to brush them off.

"Amazing to have hired an Oxford-educated tutor at the last moment," Feng marveled. "Some men have all the luck."

Nick slid one hand behind her on the small of her back. His palm, a hot brand she was proud to wear.

"What faculty were you in?" Liu asked.

She swallowed the last drops of champagne, tipping her glass vertically with a flourish. "Education," she answered. That sounded right. She was pretty sure that's what Mary had studied.

"I did a minor in Education," Liu cut in with excitement.

Her stomach flipped and she faltered against the steady hand behind her.

"Brilliant. Did you have Mr. Peabody?" She picked the most British name she could think of and just leaned in.

The brothers exchanged glances, shaking their heads.

"I'll always remember being dropped off for Michaelmas Term—best part of the year, I say," Feng concluded.

"Yes, I used to spend all summer looking forward to September." Rose shot another winning smile at her audience. This was getting easier.

"You mean October?" Feng clarified.

"Don't try and trip me up." She laughed, nervous.

A few more blundering references to Harry Potter and she felt sick to her stomach. The last joke about house dinners did not land well. Champagne and lies were a dangerous combination.

"Who did you say your favorite professor was?" Feng asked, an edge growing in his tone.

One Oxford professor, surely I can think of one Oxford professor. "Mr. Johnston-Man?"

"Johnston-Man?" Feng scoffed. The brothers switched into a rapid conversation in Chinese, the elder brother gesturing with his hands, then turning to her. "Are you saying, miss, that you attended Oxford College?"

"What are you implying?" Nick jumped in, voice terse.

"I don't believe you, but I am curious as to why you'd lie about it. Shall we continue the farce?"

"Excuse you—" Nick started.

"You know she attended Oxford *Brooks* College?" It was Alix who calmed the group, saving the day with a reference to another college.

The lined faces of the men relaxed. "Brooks? Ha, what a story," said Liu, signaling for another refill. "Quite the misunderstanding."

What a story indeed. Rose flashed a strained smile at her charge. "Canapés."

Sixteen

"You didn't go to Oxford."

A waiter sped past Nick in a vain effort to offer some privacy. It didn't matter.

She stood, shoulders back, blinking three times in quick succession. "No." Blink. Blink. "Not really. I guess I didn't."

Somewhere in his mind, Nick recognized his anger was disproportionate. Yes, lying was bad. Yes, he was her employer and there would be consequences. But what he felt now? It was akin to rage. He'd trusted her, fallen for her…

His voice shook despite his efforts to keep it measured. "*Not really?* Pick a side, Mary, either you did or you didn't."

Mary stood, and teetered back and forth.

"Didn't, then." She sounded proud of herself, perhaps for not hesitating with her answer.

He reached for her arm and pulled her toward the corner alcove. They were tucked away from prying eyes and ears, and he doubled down on his effort not to scream at her. Even through his rage he wondered, why did she have to smell so good?

"So you lied about your experience, then? Is that it? You lied?"

She pulled her arm away and rubbed a hand over her elbow where he had pulled her. But she didn't complain; instead, she brought her chin up a notch to look him in the eye. "I guess. I mean, I've *been* to Oxford. So I *went* to Oxford. I didn't *study* there, but I never claimed to."

He shook with fury. She was trying to dance around the facts with a technicality? He pressed his hands to his sides. His fingers bit into his thighs as he clenched and unclenched his fists. "That isn't the same damn thing at all."

"I guess not," she said, shoulders falling as her strong front faded. She backed up into the window seat of the alcove and sank down. Her head dropped onto her hands.

"You guess not?"

"Are you just going to repeat everything I'm saying?" Her voice quavered and her eyes filled. A curl came untucked from the pinned tower of flaxen curls on her head.

"Until I hear an apology."

"I want to explain but…" Her shoulders slumped. "Do you think I'd be better for Alix if I had a degree from a fancy-pants school?" The question was soft. He could hear the hurt in her voice. Well, that was too damn bad.

"Don't even try to turn this around on me."

"Don't try to defend myself to my lover who's so quick to think the worst of me?" Her voice caught on the word *lover* and wavered.

"Your lover? Twice, we've been together twice."

"I'm just an employee now?"

"Why don't we start with liar?" He could see that his words cut her and he continued nonetheless. All he could feel was pain and anger. He couldn't have risked the ranch on a liar. Be in love with a liar. "You've embarrassed me tonight. Badly." He paced. "You knew how important this was to me. How important Alix is to me. Anyone finds out her education is compromised and I could lose her, Mary. Lose her, lose the ranch. My sisters, Francesca—everyone is waiting for one fuckup. One mistake, and I think I just made it."

Her sharp intake of breath sliced him open.

"I can't do this right now. Can't see you right now." Then he parted the curtains and left them swishing behind him.

He was in a foul mood.

Nothing worse than being in a foul mood with a room full of people to entertain, or worse, impress. He didn't much like impressing people on a good day. Nick prowled the ballroom, shrugging off invitations and niceties as he made a beeline for the bar. "Scotch neat, the Macallan 45." He rattled off his drink order on autopilot and leaned into the leather-bound bar.

"You mean the Macallan 45, *please*," a female voice corrected. He spun and came face-to-face with the last person he expected to see, one he hadn't dared invite based on their last parting. Evie Hartmann, his sister.

"Evie!" For a moment, the room was empty, and it was just him and his little sis, together again. "It's… been a long time."

She stood back, and he took her in. Evie was twenty-eight and breathtaking. Tall, lithe and slim, she wore a sleeveless gold lamé dress and looked like a movie star from the 1950s.

"Long enough for you to change everything," she said evenly, and smiled at him as she delivered the cutting blow, reminding him she was an actress, ready and capable to deliver a line whenever the situation called for one.

"I hardly orchestrated the… Well, let's just agree it's all been very sudden, all this change." He took the Scotch off the bar, and passed it to Evie. "I'll take another," he said, then with a sidelong glance at his sister, added, "Please."

As per his usual, Ben was only moments behind Evie, and had arrived with two glasses of champagne. "I got us each a…" His voice trailed off as he took in Nick, sipping Scotch next to his sister.

Evie reached for the champagne. "Thanks." She smiled.

Nick didn't like it, not one bit. He knew his sister for

the heartbreaker that she was. Ben was too nice for her. But that was another problem for another day.

"Why did you come?" Nick drilled down to the point, his humor not sufficiently improved enough by her presence to shrug off the cloud of melancholy Mary had left him with.

"The listing agent called me." Smooth jazz flooded the room now that the band had dispensed with their break, and he struggled to hear her. "You suspended the sale? Didn't even pick up the phone to call me?" She was mad.

"I had a lot on my plate."

"Mom told me. Precisely why I'm pissed." She clamped a hand on his shoulder and squared herself to him. "You didn't call me *once* after our brother died."

"I was probably busy listening to all the voice mails you'd left me," he snapped sarcastically.

"If you're trying to figure out which Hartmann has the harder head, after a lifetime of experience, I still don't know." Ben's affable tone did little to calm the siblings.

"Too busy making friends with the niece to think of your sister? Or were you preoccupied with another set of legs?" Evie was back to being mean.

"This place is Alix's birthright, and I'm not about to parcel it up to sell to the highest bidder."

"Easy, Nick, no one's trying to sell anything," Ben said.

"This isn't over between you and me," Evie said.

But before she could issue more threats, Ben extended a hand and said, "I think you owe me a dance."

He'd let Ben deal with Evie. He'd had enough of temperamental women for the evening.

Rose stayed in the alcove for nearly forty minutes. Not crying, barely. She'd deserved the lecture. Deserved the inquisition. Deserved worse.

"You're a liar," she whispered, pinching herself, hard, finding comfort in the sharp pain. She closed her eyes, and when she reopened them moments later, she wasn't alone.

"Canapés," the small voice ventured. Rose's head jerked up.

"Canapés," she answered.

Alix stood, one hip cocked in an awkward posture, and grinned. "I did good, huh?" she asked, referencing her save during the conversation with the Shenghen brothers.

Rose smiled. "Yeah, you sure did." In a way, it was a relief to drop the facade. To put her energy into just *being*, versus trying to constantly maintain a state of perfection. "You wanna sit?" She moved over and made a bit of space on the window seat. Alix sat and Rose dived in. "I guess you know—"

"Everything," Alix finished.

There was a window in the alcove, and though the space was lit only by the stars, it was bright enough to see a corner of Alix's mouth turn up in pride. *She was so like her uncle.*

Alix shifted in her seat, and brought her big brown eyes to an inquisitive focus on Rose. "Everything... except why?"

"Then let me start at the beginning."

And so she did. Rose told Alix about a young girl who very much looked up to her sister. About an older sister who inherited an even bigger responsibility the night their parents died. About how that older sister died. She told Alix about the kids in India, her sister's legacy. She admitted that maybe the wrong sister died. A truth she'd never spoken aloud.

The one despair she didn't voice was the loss she'd earned tonight. She'd lied to Nick, when he'd been unbelievably honest with her. She didn't deserve him. But she wanted to—needed to—deserve him.

What would Mary do? And could Rose do it on her own?

"Yeah, but how did you end up here?" Alix's voice was quiet but steady.

"It's simple, really." Rose smiled, confident in the one part of this decision she'd made on her own. "I came for you."

Seventeen

She'd left the letter on purpose, putting it where he'd be sure to find it. He reckoned as much, anyway. Alix wasn't the type of kid to leave her things around; the girl was so private he'd worried at first about the lack of adolescent sprawl at the ranch. So when he retired after the gala to pour a congratulatory drink, he had been shocked to see the letter there, on the center of his desk. The placement, so deliberate. The white envelope addressed, Alix Hartmann. The letter, open underneath it.

> Alix,
> We haven't spent much time together.
> I'd like the opportunity to get to know you better, a lot better, in fact, and my lawyer tells me

at sixteen you're old enough to make the choice yourself. This is something he and I would very much like to discuss with you.

Your aunt,

Franny

Wow. Just wow. *We haven't spent much time together.* What did that even mean? From the interactions between their lawyers, he could guess at Franny's endgame. But why had Alix left the letter for him to read?

If there was one person who might have insight as to the why, it was Mary. But he couldn't go find her now—he looked down at his watch and cursed, three a.m. already? And not after the words they'd exchanged earlier this evening.

There was nothing to be done until morning. Nothing but drink more. Alone.

The first glass had gone down smooth. He read the letter again. Thought about his brother, now dead. About Katherine, the woman who'd betrayed him, who'd—indirectly—given him Alix. Thought about the woman he loved, who'd lied to him. Third glass. Another read. Another glass.

"Nick?"

Was he hallucinating? It was Mary.

"I'm glad you're awake."

Was he?

"I'm sorry—" her voice cracked "—I'm sorry about the lie." He heard the rustle of silk as she moved to stand behind him.

The fire, lit by some overeager staff member, was

now coals. Nick was transfixed by the live embers, still emanating waves of heat.

"The letter on the table—Alix left it here for me to read. Franny is openly challenging my bid for custody. You, Alix—everything is falling apart." *Everything except the deal.* He had a handshake agreement that would triple the profits of their ranch. Under his guidance, they'd become one of the most profitable cattle ranches in America. An empire, with no one who wanted it. An empire, and only him left to appreciate it.

"I didn't go to my brother's funeral. Did I ever tell you that?" He didn't move from the couch. The room was so quiet he heard the silk slide against the leather and imagined her shoulders rising to affect the pull of fabric.

"Why not?"

He directed his attention from the memory of her shoulders back to the fire. He spoke robotically, mouth set in grim determination. "I was mad at him. Still. Sixteen years later and I was mad."

"That's quite the grudge." A hand furtively descended to his shoulder.

"Katherine was my first love, but was a wild child. Wanted to leave Montana, not just for school, but forever. We fought and she broke up with me. Went with Austin to prom, even though she was my prom date."

"You'd said."

"We'd been together four years. And she slept with him on a whim that night. She said she loved me, but she lied."

Mary didn't say anything, so he continued.

"She got pregnant. I can't call it a mistake—that baby

was Alix. But I couldn't forgive her. Couldn't look at Austin. And I missed out on it all."

She swallowed, and he heard it. She had to understand. Had to see why he could never forgive her.

"You let me believe the lie, so I can't trust you. I won't... I don't even know you now."

"I guess you don't," she said with a calm so quiet he twisted to look at her. "But you could get to know me. Where I went to school, why I pretended to go to Oxford. That can't be the deal breaker here." Her voice was quiet, hopeful and heartbreaking.

"We're past deal breakers, Mary. You're a risk now. A liability." This ranch was all he had. And Alix? The one person who stood a chance at helping him keep it. If Franny were to find out that he'd misrepresented Alix's education to the courts?

"I guess you know what you want, then," she said flatly, then spun on her heel and left. She was a dichotomy. She was light. And for a moment, he'd believed he could have her.

All the more fool he. Some people, himself included, were not built for love.

She awoke before her alarm, unsure whether to blame a busy mind or her fitful sleep. Perhaps one element was responsible for the other; she couldn't know which was to blame.

Except now? For her? She knew exactly who to blame.

Rose pulled her covers off and slipped on yoga pants and a sweatshirt, the first ensemble that came to hand. Hesitating, she circled back to her dresser and grabbed for her swimsuit. One last swim before she left. It seemed appropriate, even if she hadn't earned it.

The walk to her spot at the creek was cathartic. The damp in the air smelled fresh, and the birds sang with an optimism that gave her hope all wasn't lost. She needed her five minutes, then she'd make a plan.

A plan to deserve him.

A plan to convince him that she was a risk he wanted to take.

She arrived and dialed, phone pressed to her ear, tears held back. She waited for the answer, for the recording she cherished. Then a damning beep greeted her, followed by the accursed, "I'm sorry, the number you have called has been disconnected. Please check and try again."

Disconnected? How was that even possible?

The question floated in her head, and she bit the inside of her cheek hard because she knew. The copper taste of blood startled her, but she bit down harder. By reflex, she kicked her foot against the base of the rock, then cried out in pain. It hurt. *Good.*

She hadn't paid the phone bill. Too busy falling for a rancher, preparing for a ball. Hot tears streamed down her face. "I'm sorry, Mary," she said to no one in particular. "I guess I haven't changed at all."

No sense in staying here. She now knew it with the certainty that she knew her own name. She'd failed Alix, who stood to lose the guardian and home she'd come to love, all because of her lies. She'd failed the kids in India, failed Mary's memory. She deserved to lose this place, this man. She'd go back to being a barmaid; at least she couldn't crush anyone's hopes and dreams that way.

One last swim and then she'd say goodbye.

He had almost blown it off. Almost rolled over and given in to his hangover, when the shriek of his alarm ruined his dream. And what a dream it had been! Mary, squirming against him, hot body pressed against his. But he'd pulled himself out of bed and to the creek. The cold of the swimming hole doing little to ease the memory of her. He closed his eyes. Mary was his lover in a dream, and in waking? She was a liar.

When he opened his eyes, he blinked. She was there, at the edge of the creek bank.

She wore a simple one-piece, black and efficient. It did the job with little room for vanity, but damn, even in the modest swimsuit she was a vision. A lying vision, sure, but a vision nonetheless.

She stepped into the water, ankle-deep, and shivered. After a moment's pause, she dived in.

He swam toward her, questions hot on his lips. "Didn't think I'd see you again so soon."

She didn't seem surprised to see him there. "I came to say goodbye," she started.

The statement came as no surprise. She had to leave. They were at a moral impasse, and as much as he longed to pretend it didn't matter, it did.

"Goodbye, Mary," he said simply. Nick fought the impulse to reach for her, beg her to stay. She didn't make a move to swim away just yet. He scoffed—why would she? She'd only just arrived for the swim.

"It's Rose."

The admission came from nowhere. "Rose?"

She nodded. "Mary was my sister," she choked out.

"Your sister?" He wanted to scream.

She'd been telling a bigger lie than he'd imagined. But why come clean at all? She was leaving. What did it matter if he knew everything?

"Mary died. Because of me. She was picking me up from a party, and a drunk driver… I guess it doesn't even matter. I came here because I wanted to help. I wanted to be good, like her. I read about Alix—I thought I could be there for her, two orphans. Support her, but I've messed it all to hell. I'm so sorry, Nick."

The lies were too much.

His love for her? An exquisite torture, because he felt it still.

She'd played him. And still he wanted her.

"Why did you tell me?" he asked.

"I had to," she said simply. "I love you."

The admission was directed toward the woods. She didn't look his way as she said it. Instead, she stepped out of the creek, picked up her sweatshirt and pants and walked away.

Eighteen

She'd endured a crap flight, mostly due to the fact that she'd taken the first available connection to Denver, then spent seven hours waiting for a puddle-hopper to Heathrow. It was easier waiting at the airport, staring out of focus into space, than being at his ranch fighting the feeling that she was already home.

"Here's the post." Ellen gestured toward a huge stack of envelopes as she welcomed Rose back. "I'm dying to hear all about your cowboy adventure." Ellen was smoking. Inside the flat.

"Could you not?" Rose gestured toward the cigarette.

"Sorry, did you want one?" Ellen grabbed her purse and dug through it.

"Do I want one? No." She was tired. Tired and devastated. "What I want is a nap."

Ellen got the hint. "I'll take this outside. We can get together for lunch?"

"Perfect." Rose yawned. Her arms stretched above her, and as she let them drop back to her sides, they slapped the protruding kitchen countertop that came within a meter of her entrance. How quickly she'd forgotten the "smallness" of her kitchen, particularly when faced with the vast beauty of Montana.

After five minutes stretched atop her covers, it dawned on her that she couldn't sleep.

Hope you got home okay. Thinking of you, Rose!

The text was from Alix. Checking in. She smiled at her phone and sent back an affirming, Yes, everything fine, just long. I'm knackered now but will catch up after a quick nap.

Nothing from Nick. She supposed it wasn't unexpected. They had slept together twice. Never had a simple qualifier made her feel so unimportant.

She swung her feet from the bed to the floor and made her way to the stack of correspondence with a newfound urge to be organized. She'd tackle the overdue bills and make a real plan. It probably wasn't Nick she missed, but wanting to make a difference, and she could surely find a way to do that.

It wasn't Nick she missed.

If she said it enough, maybe she'd start to believe it.

Perhaps she hadn't earned enough to sponsor all twenty-seven kids, but she had saved enough to sponsor more than half, and it was a good start. She would find another way to earn the rest of the money.

After the tenth bill, her optimism about the savings she'd tucked aside began to flicker. While she did see many opportunities to curb her spending, the large stack spoke to more than her financial obligations. Well, this was the start of it, then, of being a real grown-up. *I'm my own conscience now.*

Midstack, she pulled at a cream-colored envelope, the return address marked as Royal London Insurance. Her sister's life insurance.

Her hands shook as she opened the envelope. The letter inside was simple. Sorry about her loss. They've processed the claim. She was the named beneficiary. The sum of… "Blimey." She dropped the letter.

No, that couldn't be right. Eight hundred thousand pounds?

The forty quid Mary had set aside every month? Quite the investment indeed.

She reached for her jacket, and drove to the only place in London that made sense to her right now.

When she arrived, she stared at the headstone. It felt the same yet different. She was closer to Mary, physically, but she missed talking to her sister in the quiet of the Montana woods. The dampish cool of the stone she sat on and the alluring promise of a hard shoulder only a few minutes' cry away. Still, that was then, this was now. She had to stay in the now.

"It's an awful lot of money. What am I meant to do with it all? Did you think, if a tragedy struck, I'd be happier with the cash? Reward for good behavior?" Her voice rose and a woman ushered a young girl quickly past her to another part of the cemetery. "What should I do, then? With more money than I'd earn in ten years?"

"Those things ever talk back to you?"

She jumped at the voice. It was a gardener, or at least a man who looked like a gardener, tending to the plot a few rows behind her. He was several decades her senior, his face weathered by too much time in the sun.

"No," she admitted.

"You know what you're gonna do? With your awful lot of money?" he insisted.

She was incredulous. "You were listening?"

"You weren't whispering," he defended. "Blokes like me have to pass the time as best we can, isn't that right?" He smiled at her and her defenses slid.

"I'm sorry." She pointed to the headstone. "I just wish I could talk to her."

"Don't apologize." He rose from his plot, but to her relief turned away from her. "I still talk to my wife. I take her with me everywhere."

"But you're here," Rose said, unsure of where this conversation was going.

"Did you ever think, all we gotta do is just live honorably?" He took another few steps, then waved at her before leaving.

Live honorably. She knelt at the head of the grave and brushed the headstone free of debris. The odd twig and a few leaves had gathered at the base.

"I'm gonna make you proud, Mary," she promised.

It started to rain on her as she walked back toward

her car. She was so tired her vision blurred, and a lone tear fell on her cheek. Tears? Rain? Fatigue? It didn't matter.

I have an idea I wanted to talk over with you. Can we chat?

It wasn't smart, her idea. But as she stood, in the rain, feeling more alone than she had ever felt in her whole life, she pressed Send and sent her missive into the waiting inbox of Saul Kellerman.

Nineteen

"Please scan and send this to Jeff." Nick passed the Chinese distribution agreement to Carly, Samantha's replacement.

Samantha was doing well in her new position, and he was relieved that she'd seemed to move past her crush on him. Relieved because it felt like less of a big deal now that he was entirely unable to move past his own feelings regarding a certain British tutor.

He couldn't stop thinking about Rose. If Samantha could forgive him for his mistake, surely he could do the same?

He spun on his chair, taking in the view of the countryside he loved so dearly. He wanted to be riding, not stuck here, managing the minutia. He needed to ride the land while he still could. Who knew where the custody battle would leave him.

Not for the first time, he frowned. If he lost the custody battle, he'd lose more than the ranch. He'd lose Alix, just like he'd lost Rose. The thought of losing both the women he'd come to love suddenly a thousand times worse than losing the land he'd been fighting for.

Rose said she'd come here to help Alix. Her eagerness to do something good for her sister's memory had led to mistakes.

He studied the horizon, his own mistakes—with his brothers, his family, with Alix…with Rose—playing like an old-time movie, burning into the back of his brain. Overhead, an eagle flapped easy wings as he flew, then a second eagle joined, and the two birds hunted in tandem. Two souls, on the same journey.

Maybe love didn't mean not making mistakes. Maybe love was forgiveness. More than that, a commitment to stay regardless of mistakes. If Austin had stayed, where would they be now? One thing was for sure, if Nick had forgiven him, they'd be better still.

He wasn't sure how long he sat like that, thinking about Austin, and swallowing the regret at waiting too long to forgive, but when Evie entered, flanked by their mother and Ben, he pulled himself together. He decided that this time *he'd* forgive first.

It would hurt less than losing the chance to love.

"We are concerned," his mother started.

"*Concerned* feels like a strong word," Ben corrected.

"Strong? Not strong enough, I'd say." Evie stepped

in front of the two others and put a large manila envelope on his desk. Department of Education was written
in large capital letters.

"We think it would help everything, in particular
the custody battle plainly on the horizon, if Alix sits
an assessment test."

"Assessment test? She's had the best tutor money
could buy." He paused, realizing he meant it. Maybe
not academically, but while Mary—Rose—had been
here, Alix had transformed from a sullen teenager to a
member of the family, and he knew to whom the credit
was due. Alix had even left the letter from Franny to
help in the custody battles she knew were looming.

"Are you sure you're not being unduly influenced
by the tutor?" This time it was Josephine.

Nick didn't answer. He picked up the envelope. He
could see the point. If Alix did well on the test, it would
solidify the argument that she belonged with him, here.
That he'd made good choices for her, as her guardian.
No one had said it—no one had accused him outright
of sleeping with the tutor—but the doubt was there.
Rose was too pretty. Too tempting. No one thought he'd
hired her for Alix, and while they might be right with
regard to how it had ended, that certainly wasn't how
it had started. It had all started for Alix.

"I don't want to talk about this without Alix. As far
as I'm concerned, she gets to be a part of this conversation."

"I'm here." Her voice was small, but she stepped in
from behind the door to his office. She was dressed

simply, in jeans and a T-shirt. For the first time since she'd arrived at the ranch, her hair was pulled back off her face, in the same messy-bun style Rose had worn every day. It made her look both younger and older at the same time.

"She's gone, anyway—Rose, I mean."

"I thought it was Mary?" Evie asked.

"Anyway, she's gone now." Alix's eyes were downcast and she stared at her feet.

This admission caused a flurry of commotion, which Alix interrupted. "I'll take the test, then, whenever. Like, now is fine for me—not like you can study for an aptitude test."

"Right, that's a good point," Nick added.

"It's going to go well, Uncle Nick, don't worry. Rose did a good job."

Uncle Nick. He smiled for the first time since Rose had left.

"I wasn't worried, Alix."

The two weeks since Alix had taken the test were excruciating.

He thought about Rose every time he closed his eyes. Every time he sat on the couch, or ate dinner. Thinking about her was as natural as breathing, the impulse as hard to deny. She had been the light in his day, and everything was a crushing gray without her. He needed her back. Lies be damned.

She'd come clean when she hadn't needed to. Admitted to a bigger deception than he'd suspected. Why would she do that?

Because she loves me.

Could he forgive her?

He didn't have a choice. He loved her. But he had to wait for Alix's test results before he could leave to get her back. Rose wouldn't want him to abandon Alix when she was uncertain that she could stay.

Nick paced the hall, footsteps clicking on the polished granite floors of the foyer. The mail was here. An official-looking envelope, arriving via express service. Speedy turnaround one of the perks of a pushy lawyer and a private assessment center.

Alix's laughter echoed through the hallway as the side door pushed open and she entered with Evie. His sister was a poor substitute for Rose, but it was…nice having Evie at home again.

"Your results—they're here," he called down the hallway.

Alix's voice echoed back, "Let's read 'em over breakfast?"

They all made their way into the dining room, and once they'd sat down, she reached for a roll and dug into the food. Her face was windburned from horseback riding and she looked happy.

Nick nodded at the envelope. "Well, then?"

"You don't seem worried," Evie added, smiling.

"I'm not worried." Alix scooped a scone from the passing platter, and added it to her plate, nestling it beside the pyramid of new potatoes.

"Love the confidence, girl." Evie smiled.

Nick, impatient, opened the envelope and read aloud.

Mr. Hartmann,

Per the Montana Connect Assessment Center aptitude test and curriculum grid, it is our finding that Miss Alixandra Hartmann exceeds state standards in both Mathematics and Language Arts, with an elevated result in critical reasoning.

Please get in touch regarding tailored learning opportunities befitting her advanced placement level.

Regards,

Aurora Sinclaire

The room was thick with silence, apart from the sound of Alix's smacking lips. "These eggs are something else," she said through a mouthful of breakfast.

"Manners, Alix," Nick managed to say, head spinning from the short letter, and fingers shaking as he flipped through the attached report. *Exemplary. Exceeds peer result. Above average logic and verbal reasoning...* Every section scored with high marks. "How do you explain this?" He hoped Alix could make sense of it. The headmistress from her former school had described her as a disengaged troublemaker.

"Rose. She just made me want to try." She sliced another bit of egg.

"But I never saw you reading. You're always listening to music, disconnected..." He tried not to sound incredulous.

"Audiobooks, I'm listening to audiobooks. And podcasts on the economy."

"The economy?" Evie asked, similarly open-mouthed in shock.

"Well, yeah, but I also listen to podcasts on mental math, speed reading strategies, tons of other stuff..."

"So this whole time you've been working on advanced subjects?"

"I guess," she said, mumbling through her food. "Rose really inspired me to get curious. I wanted her to stay."

"Okay, well, I guess that's perfect." He smiled.

"Perfect?" Alix brightened. "She's coming back?"

"If she says yes." Two weeks without her was more than enough to convince him he couldn't manage a day longer. He smiled. "But I meant that with results like these, there's no question she was a good hire. That I made a good choice for you. And that you'll be able to stay."

She smiled back at him.

He was going to keep Alix. And the ranch—he had a plan for that. And Rose, too, if he could convince her to give him another chance.

But first, he had to break the news to the rest of his family.

He was nervous. It was a big step, but a necessary one. No turning back.

But he was sure. Leading this family involved change. And before he could ask Rose to spend her life with him, he needed to mend the fences he'd carelessly broken over the years.

"Thanks for meeting me. I decided I would list the

ranch—well, part of it, anyway. If y'all want. We could parcel a section. With the profits we're due to get over the next twenty-four months from the export deal, earnings are through the roof. The company can buy out the personal shares of whoever wants to sell. So if you all wanna sell. I can—" his voice cracked "—I can accept that."

The women sat in stunned silence.

"Where is this coming from?" Alix asked.

He looked at her. Fresh-faced, clever, independent. He wanted her to love this ranch, yes, but he felt ashamed that his initial motive had been a calculated one. He trusted her to make up her own mind about what was right.

"Some might think I took you in because I wanted your vote." He reddened. "Well, I did want your vote. But more than that, I want you. You're my family. And you're smart. A lot smarter than any of us gave you credit for. You get a say in what you want."

Alix pushed her chair closer to him. "Uncle Nick," she said plainly. "I'm not going to sell."

Evie spoke next, following Alix's overture with a light cough. "You know, I'm kinda liking Montana these days. I was thinking maybe I could take over the old house? You know, official-like?"

Nick felt a wide smile spread across his face. "You wanna stay?" Incredible that he'd gone from being the only Hartmann to care about this ranch to one of many.

Amelia spoke for the first time. "I'm not selling, either. Now that I'm divorcing…"

His head spun. "Wait. You both want—"

"We *all* want to be included in how this ranch is run," Josephine corrected, smiling. "It's our legacy. Our *family's* legacy. Thanks for making us a part of the process."

Nick rubbed a hand over his eyes, giving himself a second to blink away his surprise, eyes hot with emotion. He opened his mouth to speak, then shut it, instead studying his family. Evie, arm slung over Amelia's shoulders, hand rubbing her back with a steady and reassuring pace. Josephine, focused on Alix, who beamed back at him, eyes dancing and mouth wide in a smile. Jackson would always have his back, but to feel the support of the other members of his family was a dream come true. All the Hartmanns aligned, and just one person was missing from the equation. An English rose.

Twenty

When Nick arrived at the door of her apartment, un-shaven and mildly disheveled, he knocked before he could think twice.

He was here for her, and he didn't want to waste one more moment waiting.

"You're late," she said simply after opening the door.

"I came as fast as I could," he answered. "Can I come in?" He took his hat off and held it to his chest like armor.

Alix had opted to stay in the café next door, and Nick was grateful that she understood the tact he would need to dig himself out of his current predicament. While he was ready to grovel, he preferred to do it without witnesses.

"I guess." Rose stepped back and let him in.

Her flat was disordered, mostly due to the cartons filling every available space.

"Moving?" he asked, gesturing around.

"Yep," she shot back. "I'm downsizing. In my new job, I plan to travel."

"New job?"

She shifted against the doorframe. "Would you like a cuppa?" Rose waved toward her kitchen.

"I would," he said, more to appease her than because he wanted tea.

She turned, and in two paces was in the corner of her flat designated as a kitchen.

"Where are you off to, then?" He shifted. He hadn't come for small talk, but couldn't seem to find a way to say what he'd come to say.

"I've still got a bit to figure out, but I'm starting a charity."

"A charity?" He edged closer to her and put his hat on the small counter dividing the cooking area from the dining area.

"Look, Nick. I know I messed everything up. But getting to know Alix, getting to know you…getting to *matter* to someone? It helped me, Nick. And now? I just want to do it again."

He bit down on his lip. *He had a chance.*

She continued, fingers squeezing into fists and clenched at her sides. "I took the life insurance money. From Mary. I had no idea about the policy, but it's enough to make a difference. I've incorporated a nonprofit. I want to offer inner-city kids a chance to reconnect with nature. To heal, away from the pressures of the city, to commune with horses, to swim in a creek… Saul Kellerman is helping me set it up. He mentioned there might be some land for sale. In Montana." She pushed a curl back from her face, tucking it behind her ear, and for a minute he swore his pulse stopped.

She looked at him, raising her eyes to meet his. "I'm so sorry, Nick. I didn't take the job to fall in love with you, but I fell…hard. And yes, I lied about my name and my education, but I have never been more myself than I was with you these past few months. How I felt about you? It's the most honest thing I've ever felt in my life. I love you. Love your land. I love Alix." Her voice caught.

He took a step toward her, but she held up a hand to stop him. "I want to be near you. Show you I'm good. Earn back your trust. I'm ready to invest everything I have. Everything I am." The timbre of her voice fell, and she added a soft, "Do you think it will ever be enough?"

He stepped closer to her. Crossed that invisible line between holding grudges and the willingness to forgive. Crossed into her space. "You're enough. You're so much more than enough." He took a final step, feeling his chest brush against hers, unable to stand any closer without crushing her toward him. "I'm sorry, too," he managed gruffly. "It took me a little while to make things right with the family. Or start to make them right. I mean, I'm the first to admit everyone makes mistakes, but I wanted to fix some of mine. I've made enough of them."

"You can say that again," she whispered, then paled. "I meant, that everyone makes mistakes." She followed the sentiment with a playful pat to his chest, but he caught her hand and pressed it over his heart.

He wasn't going to let himself off the hook that easily. He didn't want to. He wanted to give her everything she deserved, and that started with the truth.

She stiffened, pulling back from him. "Why are you here, Nick?"

"It's simple," he started, realizing for the first time that it was.

Sure, he'd made things right with his siblings, but he'd be here even if that wasn't the case. He'd rather be here, with her, than anywhere else in the world alone.

"I've never loved anyone as much as I love you. You took Alix, my kin, my friends, and you made us a home. You made us a family. You're complicated, genuine, beautiful, delightfully defiant, endlessly sexy and… I need you. I love you. Utterly. Completely. I didn't care when I left, didn't care if I was gonna be too late, I had to come. I had to try. I had to tell you. You want to know why I came?" The words escaped him, traveling on the last breath he had. That was the thing about it all. If he could use a last breath for anything it would be to say, "I love you." So he did.

She nodded, eyes shining.

"And so?" he continued. "Do you think you have enough charity left in you to forgive a fool of a cowboy?"

"It depends." She smiled and let her hands circle his neck. "Does a *Rose* by any other name taste as sweet?"

Nick Hartmann was thirty-two. He might not know everything, but somehow he'd gotten everything he ever wanted. And when it came to the answer to this age-old question, first posed by Shakespeare, he was confident.

She did.

* * * * *

Don't miss Katie Frey's next Western,
coming Fall 2022!

And if you liked Montana Legacy,
check out these other Westerns from
Harlequin Desire!

Return of the Rancher
by USA TODAY *bestselling author Janice Maynard*
Available now!

and

Rocky Mountain Rivals
by Joanne Rock
Available May 2022

WE HOPE YOU ENJOYED
THIS BOOK FROM

DESIRE

*Luxury, scandal, desire—welcome to
the lives of the American elite.*

Be transported to the worlds of oil barons, family dynasties,
moguls and celebrities. Get ready for juicy plot twists,
delicious sensuality and intriguing scandal.

6 NEW BOOKS AVAILABLE EVERY MONTH!

#2875 BOYFRIEND LESSONS

Texas Cattleman's Club: Ranchers and Rivals
by Sophia Singh Sasson

Ready to break out of her shell, shy heiress Caitlyn Lattimore needs the help of handsome businessman Dev Mallik to sharpen her dating skills. Soon, fake dates lead to steamy nights. But can this burgeoning relationship survive their complicated histories?

#2876 THE SECRET HEIR RETURNS

Dynasties: DNA Dilemma • by Joss Wood

Secret heir Sutton Marchant has no desire to connect with his birth family or anyone else. But when he travels to accept his inheritance, he can't ignore his attraction to innkeeper Lowrie Lewis. Can he put the past behind him to secure his future?

#2877 ROCKY MOUNTAIN RIVALS

Return to Catamount • by Joanne Rock

Fleur Barclay, his brother's ex, should be off-limits to successful rancher Drake Alexander, especially since they've always despised one another. But when Fleur arrives back in their hometown, there's a spark neither can ignore, no matter how much they try...

#2878 A GAME BETWEEN FRIENDS

Locketts of Tuxedo Park • by Yahrah St. John

After learning he'll never play again, football star Xavier Lockett finds solace in the arms of singer Porscha Childs, until a misunderstanding tears them apart. When they meet again, the heat is still there. But they might lose each other once more if they can't resolve their mistakes...

#2879 MILLION-DOLLAR CONSEQUENCES

The Dunn Brothers • by Jessica Lemmon

Actor Isaac Dunn needs a date to avoid scandal, and his agent's sister, Meghan Squire, is perfect. But pretending leads to one real night... and a baby on the way. Will this convenient arrangement withstand the consequences—and the sparks—between them?

#2880 CORNER OFFICE CONFESSIONS

The Kane Heirs • by Cynthia St. Aubin

To oust his twin brother from the family company, CEO Samuel Kane sets him up to break the company's cardinal rule—no workplace relationships. But it's *Samuel* who finds himself tempted when Arlie Banks awakes a passion that could cost him everything...

SPECIAL EXCERPT FROM

(H) HARLEQUIN

DESIRE

*Focused on finishing an upcoming album, sound
engineer Teagan Woodson and guitarist Maxton McCoy
struggle to keep things professional as their attraction
grows. But agreeing to "just a fling" may lead to
everything around them falling apart...*

Read on for a sneak peek at
After Hours Temptation
by Kianna Alexander.

Maxton eyed Teagan and asked, "Isn't there something I didn't get to see?"

She smiled. "If you mean my bedroom, you gotta earn it, playboy."

"Sounds like a challenge," he quipped.

She shook her head. "No. More of a requirement."

He laughed, then gently dragged the tip of his index finger along her jawline. "You're going to make me work for this. I just know it."

Her answer was a sultry smile. "We'll just have to see what happens."

"Truth is, I really don't have the time for a relationship right now."

If she took offense at his statement, she didn't show it. "Neither do I."

"So, what are we doing here?"

She shrugged. "A fling? A dalliance? I don't think it really matters what we call it, so long as we both understand what it is…and what it isn't."

Their gazes met and held, and the sparkle of mischief in her eyes threatened to do him in. "Enlighten me, Teagan. What will we be doing, exactly?"

"We hang out…have a little fun. No strings, no commitments. And, above all, we don't let this thing interfere with our work or our lives." She pressed her open palm against his chest. "That is, if you think you can handle it."

"Seems reasonable." *I like this approach. Seems like we're on one accord.*

Her smile deepened. "Tomorrow is my only other free day for a while. Why don't you meet me at the Creamery, right near Piedmont Park? Say around seven?"

"I'll be there." He wanted to kiss her but couldn't read her thoughts on the matter. So he grazed his fingertip over her soft glossy lips instead.

"See you then," she whispered.

Satisfied, he opened the front door and stepped out into the afternoon sunshine.

Don't miss what happens next in…
After Hours Temptation
by Kianna Alexander.

Available June 2022 wherever
Harlequin Desire books and ebooks are sold.

Harlequin.com

Love Harlequin romance?

DISCOVER.

Be the first to find out about promotions, news and exclusive content!

Facebook.com/HarlequinBooks

Twitter.com/HarlequinBooks

Instagram.com/HarlequinBooks

Pinterest.com/HarlequinBooks

You Tube YouTube.com/HarlequinBooks

ReaderService.com

EXPLORE.

Sign up for the Harlequin e-newsletter and download a free book from any series at **TryHarlequin.com**

CONNECT.

Join our Harlequin community to share your thoughts and connect with other romance readers!
Facebook.com/groups/HarlequinConnection

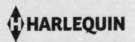

HSOCIAL2021

HARLEQUIN

Heartfelt or thrilling, passionate or uplifting—Harlequin is more than just happily-ever-after.

With twelve different series to choose from and new books available every month, you are sure to find stories that will move you, uplift you, inspire and delight you.